COUNT THE

AUTHOR'S NOTE

All the 'mugging' and 'robbery with violence' there is today in every country may be due to the leniency with which the modern Highwayman and footpads are treated.

The records of Newgate prison show that two footpads who stopped a journeyman tailor near Harrow and robbed him of two pence and his clothes, were executed. Tom Lympus a Highwayman was successful for several years in robbing the mails, with a reward of two hundred pounds on his head. He was finally caught and hanged.

John Ram commonly called Sixteen Strong Jack was a very colourful character. Women adored him and when he was finally brought to trial he was dressed in a new suit of pea-green, a ruffled shirt and his hat was bound with silver string. He was ordered to be executed but the night before he had seven girls to dine with him and the company was reported to be remarkably cheerful.

The following morning he faced the gallows

with composure and his body hung on the usual tree before being delivered to his friends for interment.

Noblemen in the 17th and 18th centuries usually were armed and travelled with outriders. A blunderbuss was carried on the Stage Coaches. Those who walked unattended on commons, fields or lonely roads lost not only their money but often their lives.

CHAPTER 1

1825

'Major Stanley, Your Grace,' the Butler announced.

The Duke of Brockenhurst put down the newspaper he had been reading and looked up expectantly.

Into the Library came a vision.

Freddie Stanley was wearing the traditional shining breastplate and high, brightly-polished riding-boots over white buckskin breeches of the Life Guards.

He had left his wide-cuffed white gloves and his flamboyant shining silver helmet with its hanging plumes, which had been invented by the King when he was Prince Regent, in the Hall.

'You dazzle me, Freddie,' the Duke exclaimed mockingly.

'Damn it all,' his friend replied, 'I got your message just as I was going on parade, and as it seemed so urgent I came the moment I was free.'

Crossing the room with his spurs tinkling he seated himself rather gingerly in an armchair opposite the Duke.

'What's all this flap-doodle?' he enquired. 'I expected to find the house burnt down, or to learn you had lost your fortune on the Exchange, although I imagine that would be impossible.'

'It is none of those things,' the Duke said in a more serious tone of voice. 'The fact is Freddie, I am bored.'

'Bored!' Freddie exclaimed. 'You do not mean to tell me you have brought me here at a gallop to tell me something I have known for the last two years.'

'You have!'

'Of course I have. It is not surprising.'

'What do you mean it is not surprising?' the Duke asked.

'I will answer that when you tell me why you have suddenly discovered what has been palpably obvious.'

The Duke shifted a little restlessly in his chair.

'I realised it last night,' he replied, 'when I knew it was impossible for me to ask Imogen to marry me.'

Freddie Stanley looked astonished.

'Are you telling me,' he asked after a distinct pause, 'that you intend to cry-off?'

The Duke nodded.

'But my dear Brock,' Freddie expostulated, 'everyone has been expecting the announcement for months. Wentover has stalled his creditors on the assumption that you will pay his debts once Imogen is your wife.'

'I suspected that,' the Duke said. 'But why the hell I should be expected to pay for Wentover's extravagances, especially the diamonds he had given that pretty Cyrian he has in tow, is past my comprehension.'

'It wouldn't have made much of a hole in your pocket,' Freddie replied briefly. 'But I do not see how you can do this at the eleventh hour.'

'I haven't actually asked her to marry me.'

'But you made it pretty obvious, pursuing her as you have.'

The Duke's lips twisted cynically as he said:

'If you ask me, I was the one pursued.'

'All right, but you did not run away,' Freddie replied. 'You gave parties for her in London and in the country, and danced with her at least four or five times at the Ball at Windsor Castle. I saw you with my own eyes.'

'I am not denying all that,' the Duke answered testily. 'What I am telling you, Freddie, is that I suddenly realised last night that, beautiful though she is, Imogen has the brains of a three-year-old child.'

'I could have told you that,' Freddie remarked laconically.

'It is a pity you refrained from doing so!'

'What was the point? You would not have listened! You were too busy using your eyes instead of your ears where she was concerned.'

'That was exactly what I realised last night!'

There was a pause, then Freddie said:

'You had better tell me about it.'

The Duke drew in his breath.

'I danced with Imogen for the third time at the Richmonds Ball and then we went into the garden. With the moon shining, the Chinese lanterns, and all the romantic trappings, I was just about to kiss her, when she said something.'

'What did she say?' Freddie asked curiously.

'I cannot really remember,' the Duke replied. 'It was something so banal—so obvious—that I was suddenly aware it was the sort of remark I would hear her make for the next fifty years, and knew I could not stand it.'

'You really might have discovered this before!'

'I know—I know,' the Duke said testily. 'But better late than never. I reiterate, Freddie, I have not asked her to marry me.'

'Then what are you going to do about it?'

'That is what I am asking you,' the Duke replied.

Freddie with some difficulty sat back further in the armchair.

'It is all very well, Brock,' he said, 'but if you do not marry Imogen, what is the alternative? In your position you have to produce an heir.'

'Plenty of time for that,' the Duke replied.

'I know, but if it is not Imogen, it will be someone very like her.'

'Good God, are you telling me all the women in the *Beau Monde* are as stupid and brainless as she is?'

'I suppose they are at that age,' Freddie said reflectively. 'As you will know, they come out of the schoolroom with only one fixed idea in their heads.'

'To get married,' the Duke finished.

'Of course—to the highest bidder—and who higher than a Duke?'

'I will not do it!' the Duke said angrily.

There was silence before Freddie replied:

'In that case, unless you are prepared to face the music, which means Wentover's anger and

Imogen's tears, you had better make yourself scarce.'

'I have been wondering most of the night if that is what I should do.'

'Where have you considered going?'

The Duke shrugged his shoulders.

'Does it matter? I own, as you well know, half a dozen houses in different parts of the country, and there is my yacht in the harbour at Folkestone.'

'I suppse you are hoping I will come with you.'

'It did enter my mind,' the Duke replied with a faint smile.

Freddie thought for a moment, and then he said:

'I think you are making a mistake.'

'By not marrying Imogen?'

'No—in running away in so obvious a fashion.'

'Damn it all! I am not running away,' the Duke answered. 'I am making a strategic withdrawal.'

Freddie laughed.

'A pretty phrase for not facing the enemy.'

'Stop jibbing at me and help me,' the Duke begged. 'That is why I have sent for you.'

He paused before he went on:

'I am well aware I am behaving in a somewhat reprehensible fashion. If Imogen would not make me a good wife, I would certainly make her a bad husband.'

'That is very true,' Freddie agreed, 'and if you ask me, marrying anyone because it is expected of you is asking for trouble.'

The Duke groaned.

'What else can I do with my relatives at me day and night, talking as if I were Methuselah and implying that in a year or so I shall be incapable of breeding?'

Freddie put back his head and laughed. Then he said:

'That is one of the few penalties of being a Duke. There are not many others.'

'I am not sure about that,' the Duke replied. 'I find myself bound by a great many restrictions which other people, like yourself, do not have to endure.'

Freddie looked at him speculatively, then he said:

'Do you want to hear the truth, Brock? Or will you find it disturbing to come out of your Cloud-Cuckoo Land?'

'Is that where you think I live?'

'I do not think—I know.'

'All right, tell me the truth—it is bound to

be unpleasant.'

'I have been thinking about you for some time,' Freddie began slowly. 'The truth is that you are too important, too handsome, too rich, too damn sure of yourself.'

'Thank you,' the Duke answered sarcastically.

'You asked me for the truth, and now you are going to hear it. It is that you are not in touch with reality, both people and the circumstances in which most of us live.'

'That is too much!' the Duke expostulated. 'What you are saying is that my life as I live it is too soft. It certainly wasn't soft when you and I were serving in Wellington's Army.'

'That was ten years ago,' Freddie replied. 'You sold out after Waterloo, when your father died, and since then you have been cosseted, acclaimed and fussed over as if you were a rare species that must be kept at all costs from the contamination of the world outside one of your Ivory Castles.'

The Duke sighed.

'I suppose you are right.'

'Just look at the way you live,' Freddie said. 'Your servants treat you as if you were a bit of Dresden china. You have Comptrollers, secretaries, agents, managers, who see to all your affairs!'

The Duke made a sound of expostulation but did not prevent Freddie from continuing:

'When they are not fawning on you and kissing your boots, there is every lovely woman in the social world yearning to go to bed with you or to marry you.'

'Do I hear a note of envy in your voice?' the Duke asked.

'It might be there if I did not know you so well,' Freddie admitted, 'but I have watched you growing more cynical, more bored every year. I have told myself a dozen times that I would rather be me than you.'

'I suppose if we were in a fairy story or a French farce,' the Duke said, 'we could change places. Wearing my clothes, you would become the Duke, and I would go clanking off back to the barracks in your place.'

'As that is not possible, I have a better idea.'

'What is it?' the Duke asked.

'First, it is quite obvious that you have to disappear. Secondly, I think it would be good for your soul, if you have one, to think about yourself and your future.'

'That is something I do quite frequently.'

'Then you will have to think again,' Freddie said firmly. 'Of how to find a different way of life from the one you are living now. You cannot go on pursuing and raising expectations in maidens' breasts, only to leave them desolate at the Church door.'

'Curse you, Freddie! It is not a thing I do often,' the Duke expostulated.

'What about Charlotte?'

'Charlotte assumed that I meant marriage,' the Duke replied. 'But, as you know, my intentions were strictly dishonourable.'

Freddie laughed.

'The one thing about you, Brock, is that you are always straightforward in your infamy.'

'The same answer applies to Louise if you were thinking of mentioning her.'

'I had no intention of doing so, as it happens,' Freddie replied. 'Louise was certainly not an innocent little flower, she knew what she wanted, and at one moment I thought she was going to get it.'

'She deceived me for quite a considerable amount of time,' the Duke admitted.

Freddie bent forward, then winced as his breastplate stuck into him.

'What are you looking for, Brock?' he asked with a serious note in his voice.

'I wish I knew,' the Duke answered. 'I just know that I am dissatisfied and, as I have already told you, unutterably bored.'

'Do you really think if we go off together to Cornwall, Wales or even Scotland you will feel any different?' Freddie asked. 'No, Brock, you would still be pampered and restricted, and when we come back to London you will be just as bored as you are now.'

'Then for God's sake tell me what I can do,' the Duke said testily.

'I doubt if you will like it.'

'I will listen to any suggestion you make to me.'

'Very well,' Freddie said. 'What I suggest is you go off alone and incognito.'

'I often travel under one of my other names,' the Duke replied.

'I did not mean calling yourself Lord Hurst, and travelling with your horses, your servants, your coachmen, your valet and a couple of out-riders,' Freddie said scornfully. 'When I said alone—I meant alone.'

The Duke looked puzzled.

'Let me explain,' Freddie went on, 'and if it makes it any easier, I will make it a wager.'

The Duke listened as his friend continued:

'I bet my Canaletto which is the only really valuable thing I possess, against your team of chestnuts, that you will not ride from here to

York, alone, unaccompanied, incognito, without giving up because it is too tough and sending for your servants and horses.'

Freddie had spoken slowly as if he was choosing every word with care.

Now the Duke was staring at him, as if he did not hear him aright.

'You will really risk your Canaletto on such an absurd bet?' he asked.'

'I have always rather fancied your chestnuts.'

'It is the most ridiculouss thing I have ever heard!' the Duke exclaimed. 'Of course I can do it if I want to, and with the greatest ease.'

'Are you refusing my challenge?'

'I am just wondering what good it will do.'

'It might give you a new angle on life, a new appreciation of living.'

'I very much doubt it,' the Duke replied. 'I imagine the roads will be dusty, the Inns in which I will stay atrocious and unless I enjoy the company of tramps and yokels, the conversation will be somewhat limited.'

'That is up to you,' Freddie said practically. 'I think you might find it an adventure.'

'I doubt it!'

The Duke rose as he spoke to walk towards the table in the corner of the Library, on which there was a profusion of drinks, a bottle of champagne in a silver wine-cooler and cut-glass decanters of madeira, sherry, brandy and claret.

'What will you have, Freddie?' he asked without turning round.

'You should have asked me before,' Freddie said. 'However since I wish to drink a toast to your future I think it should be champagne.'

'I have not said I am going to accept your ridiculous challenge.'

'Then of course I shall look forward to being best man at your wedding.'

The Duke laughed as he walked across the room with a glass of champagne in his hand.

'You are trying to push me into a tight corner. I know your tactics only too well.'

When he had given the champagne to his friend, he walked to the window to look out at the trees in Berkeley Square.

It was a sunny day, and it struck him that it was a mistake to waste the time in London when he might be in the country.

The gardens at Hurst Castle in Hampshire would be looking very beautiful, and he thought it was a long time since he had bathed in the sea from his house in Cornwall.

'Come with me, Freddie,' he said most beguilingly. 'It would be fun if we were together. At least we would be able to laugh, as we laughed in the War.'

For a moment Freddie Stanley was tempted.

It was true when the two of them had joined Wellington's Army when they were both eighteen, the privations, the hunger and danger and even the appalling casualties had been mitigated because they were together, and because nothing seemed quite so bad when it was shared.

The Duke turned round to wait for Freddie's reply.

'No,' Freddie said firmly, and his voice seemed to ring out.

'No?'

'No,' Freddie reiterated. 'You know as well as I do, Brock, I shall be running round obeying your orders, and making things better and more comfortable for you than they would be otherwise.'

He grinned as he added:

'You have got considerably more authoritative in the last ten years, but I haven't forgotten that at Waterloo you purloined my water-bottle because you had forgotten your own. I parted with it as if you had a right to it.'

'Oh, for God's sake, Freddie!' the Duke exclaimed. 'What has that got to do with it?'

'A great deal,' Freddie replied. 'It has been the same ever since. You know as well as I do it is "Freddie do this", and "Freddie do that". I obey you willingly because I am fond of you, but for once you are going to have no one to order about except your horse.'

'I wonder you do not expect me to walk to York.'

'That is an idea, but it would take too long. And quite frankly, I will miss you.'

'You are absolutely confident I shall agree to your nonsensical idea!'

'If you think it out, it is an excellent one considering all the circumstances. You will tell your household you have gone abroad, so there will be nothing Imogen can do about that, and your other subservient creatures can cancel your engagements and answer your love-letters.'

The Duke suddenly laughed.

'Freddie, you are a fool! But because you are a fool who always amuses me, I insist you come with me.'

'Chickenhearted!' Freddie asked mockingly. 'Or merely afraid that you will lose your way, as you did one misty night when your Company nearly walked into the French lines?'

'Curse you, it was not a mist but a fog,' the Duke replied. 'Anyway, I know the way to York. I have twice been to the races in Doncaster.'

'There is one more condition which I forgot to mention,' Freddie said.

'What is that?'

'You have to reach York without being recognised. If either you reveal your true identity, or you are pointed out as being the Duke, then the chestnuts are mine.'

'I assure you I have no intention of losing my horses,' the Duke replied. 'And I know exactly the right place to hang the Canaletto at the Castle.'

'It will remain empty,' Freddie said confidently. 'And I shall warn my groom to get the stables ready.'

'Damn you!' the Duke answered. 'I will prove you wrong. I will be the winner of this contest if it is the last thing I ever do.'

As he spoke he walked across the room to the wine-cooler to pick up the bottle of champagne with which to replenish his own glass and that of his friend, so he did not notice the look of satisfaction in Freddie's eyes.

No one knew better than he that the Duke had been wasting his life for the last few years among the so-called delights of the *Beau Monde*.

There were racing, mills, cock-fighting and gambling to supplement the endless round of Balls and Assemblies, Receptions, and of course the dance-halls of the Fashionable Impures with whom the noblemen spent much of their time.

Freddie had watched a young man, who had been idealistic, enthusiastic and incredibly brave, become progressively more cynical, bored and indolent, and knew that the Duke was losing something very precious.

They were both of them in their thirtieth year. While Freddie had stayed in the Regiment, the Duke on his father's death had at first been busily occupied putting his estates in order, and then he had found little to do which required his intelligence.

There were too many skilled employees to lift every possible burden from his shoulders, and as the King grew older even his hereditary duties at Court were little but a sinecure.

Freddie had thought for some time that he should do something for his closest friend, but the opportunity to speak freely had never presented itself until now.

'When do I leave on this wild-goose chase?' the Duke asked.

'As soon as possible,' Freddie replied. 'Otherwise you may be quite certain that Wentover will be knocking on your door demanding an explanation.'

The Duke looked startled.

'He could hardly take me to task for not proposing to his daughter last night.'

'Why not?' Freddie asked. 'The betting in White's is that the engagement will be announced before the end of the week.'

'Why should they assume that?'

'Because Wentover has been boasting that he will be riding your hunters this winter, and has already decided that he would be able to hunt with at least two more packs than he can now afford.'

'I have never heard such cheek!' the Duke said. 'As he weighs at least sixteen stone, I am not letting him give my horses a sore back.'

'If you stay here you will have to explain that to him in words of one syllable.'

'Very well—I will leave immediately after luncheon.'

Freddie lifted his glass.

'To your journey and may you find what you seek.'

'I am not seeking anything,' the Duke replied crossly.

Freddie opened his lips to refute this idea, and shut them again.

He rose to his feet hampered by his high riding-boots.

'I am going back to the Barracks to change,'

he said. 'If you have not gone when I return, I will say "goodbye" to you then. If not, I will sound suitably surprised by your departure. I shall also complain bitterly in the Club you did not tell me where you were going.'

The Duke, who had only taken one sip of his champagne, put his glass down on the table.

'I suppose you know that this is a crazy idea!'

'Take enough money with you to bring you home,' Freddie said. 'And remember there are always Highwaymen to take it off you.'

The Duke looked startled.

'Do you remember,' he continued, 'how the General used to tell you to be ready for anything and remember it is always likely to be the worst?'

'I remember that,' the Duke smiled. 'You are making me positively apprehensive!'

'You used to rather enjoy dangerous situations,' Freddie said reflectively. 'But I suppose now you have got old and fat...'

It wasn't possible to say any more, for the Duke had picked up a silk cushion and flung it at him.

'You are takng an unfair advantage,' he said. 'I would knock you down, but in that fancy rig you would only lie on your back like an old sheep.'

'When you return fitter than you are now,' Freddie answered. 'I will take you on and see if you can last ten rounds. At the moment I imagine you are only capable of three.'

'Get out, damn you!' the Duke exclaimed. 'I know you are only saying all this to goad me into doing what you want. Very well, Freddie, I will go to York, and if I get my throat cut on the way or die of exhaustion, I will come back and haunt you!'

'I will drive your chestnuts down to the Castle and put some flowers on your grave,' Freddie replied. 'Presumably you will be interred in the family vault!'

He did not wait to hear the Duke's reply, but went out of the Library, shutting the door behind him.

The Duke was laughing as he walked across the room to his desk. He seated himself in the high-backed chair on which was carved the Brockenhurst Coat of Arms.

Then he rang the gold bell which stood beside the gold ink-pot and opened the blotter on which his Coat of Arms appeared, again in gold.

A servant answered the bell, and the Duke asked for his Comptroller, Mr Dunham.

A middle-aged man, he had been with the

previous Duke for the last years of his life, and now served his present employer with tact, loyalty and an expertise which made everything run like a well-oiled machine.

'Morning, Dunham,' the Duke said, as he came into the room.

'Good morning, Your Grace. I have here the plans you asked for, for the constructin of a private racecourse at the Castle.'

'I have no time for that at the moment,' the Duke replied. 'I am leaving London immediately after luncheon, which I wish to be at twelve-thirty.'

'I will see to it, Your Grace. Will you be driving your Phaeton?'

'I am going on horseback, and alone,' the Duke answered.

His Comptroller looked at him incredulously, as he went on.

'As far as the household is concerned, and anyone who makes enquiries—I have gone abroad.'

'Your yacht, as you know, Your Grace, is always ready to leave harbour at an hour's notice.'

'I have not forgotten, Dunham,' the Duke said, 'but there is no need to send anyone to notify the Captain of my arrival. If I do join the yacht it will be a surprise.'

Mr Dunham looked faintly apprehensive, but did not speak.

The Duke went on:

'I want Hercules, no I think Samson, brought to the front door at one o'clock. After that you will not be able to get in communication with me, until I notify you of where I am.'

'I do not wish to sound impertinent, Your Grace,' Mr Dunham said respectfully, 'but I feel worried that you should be leaving without a groom.'

'I wish to go alone,' the Duke replied firmly, 'and I am likely to be away for two weeks, perhaps more. As I have already said, everybody is to be informed I have gone abroad.'

He knew as he spoke that his Comptroller was longing to ask him a dozen questions but was too well trained to do so.

'I shall, of course, require money,' the Duke said. 'A Letter of Credit, which will be honoured by my Bank, notes of a high denomination and, of course, enough loose sovereigns not to be an encumbrance.'

Mr Dunham made a note on the pad he held in his hand as the Duke spoke. Now he waited for any other instructions.

The Duke walked towards the door. He had almost reached it when he turned back to say:

'You have known me for a great number of years, Dunham. Would you say that I am out of condition in any way?'

The question took his Comptroller by surprise. Then as the Duke expected an immediate flattering answer Mr Dunham hesitated.

'No need to put it into words, Dunham,' the Duke said sharply and went from the room.

★ ★ ★ ★

Riding North an hour later the Duke found himself resenting the implication, both from Freddie and his Comptroller, that he was not fighting fit.

He always prided himself that unlike most of his contemporaries he was athletically in the peak of condition as he had been when he was in the Army.

Then the long hours in the saddle, the strenuous travelling over foreign and hostile country, the fighting, the never being certain when the next meal would turn up, made him almost a young Samson.

It had in fact been his nickname amongst the men with whom he served, and it was why he called one of the finest horses he had ever owned by the same name.

Samson, the black stallion he was riding now, needed all his master's strength and expertise to keep him under control.

The Duke knew, if he was honest, that despite the pugilistic bouts and fencing which he enjoyed several times a week, he had allowed himself to gain in weight and there were several more inches of flesh on his body than there had been five years ago.

He admitted Freddie had been right when he had said he was cosseted and pampered, and that he had grown to take it all for granted.

Fine linen sheets on beds that were soft as a cloud, superlative food which was served up by his Chef at every meal, claret that was brought by his Agents from the finest vineyards in France, which once again were in production after the devastation of war, were part of his routine of life and taken for granted.

Then of course, there was the softness of white arms around his neck, red lips raised willingly and usually hungrily, towards his.

'It is not really a man's life,' he told himself, 'as I should have discovered sooner. Perhaps Freddie is right, this will be an adventure in living. All the same, I doubt it!'

He could not help acknowledging, however, that when he rode away from Berkeley Square alone, without a groom in attendance, and saw the puzzled expression on the face of Mr Dunham, the Butler and five of his six-footer liveried footmen, he had felt somewhat strange.

He could not remember when he had last set off by himself without an escort.

It was impossible in a way not to regret the comfort of driving his team of perfectly matched chestnuts which Freddie had always envied.

Also if he was going to Newmarket, or to stay at any other place outside London, his Valet would have already gone ahead to have everything ready for his arrival.

If he was travelling any distance there would be two or perhaps four outriders in attendance. One of them was, if he had to stay at an Inn, an excellent cook.

Now on the road leading North, the Duke wondered if in his haste to leave London he had forgotten anything of real importance.

He had told his Valet that he required only what could be carried attached to the saddle.

'Do you mean to say, Your Grace, I am not coming with you?' Jenkins had asked incredulously.

'I will let you into a secret, Jenkins,' the Duke replied. 'I have accepted a wager and, if I am to win it, I have to look after myself.'

'You will never manage that, Your Grace.'

'What do you mean?' the Duke asked sharply. 'Just because you mollycoddle me, it does not mean to say I am helpless without you.'

He knew that was what Jenkins was thinking, as the man tightened his lips.

'What I require you to do,' the Duke went on, 'is to pack me some shirts—something comfortable I can change into when I have ridden all day—a night-shirt and my razor—impossible for me to take anything more.'

'I presume Your Grace will require fresh cravats,' Jenkins said in the triumphant tone of a servant who had found a flaw in a plan of which he disapproved.

'If I do not have everything I need,' the Duke said sharply, 'I shall be extremely annoyed when I return.'

'Your Grace had much better let me come with you,' Jenkins remarked.

The Duke did not deign to reply and merely started to change his clothes.

Instead of the close-fitting champagne-coloured knitted pantaloons he wore, he put on a heavier pair which he had not worn for some time and found they were slightly tight.

It irritated him, but he did not mention it.

Refusing the highly-polished, very elegant riding-boots, which had recently been delivered from Maxwell's in Dover Street, he chose instead an old and comfortable pair of riding-boots, which Jenkins thought he should have discarded.

The Duke was sensible enough to realise he must not appear too conspicuous, not only because he would lose his bet if he was recognised, but in case he attracted too much attention as a lone, and therefore unprotected, rider.

He slipped a small pistol into the pocket of his grey whipcord riding-jacket, and to Jenkins' disgust tied his cravat in a careless unfashionable style, which was more suitable to a country Squire than a gentleman of fashion.

When it came to choosing a hat, the Duke again picked up one that was high crowned but five years old and had been somewhat battered by the wind and the rain when he had been out shooting.

'You don't look right to me, Your Grace, and that's a fact,' Jenkins remarked.

'It is how I wish to look,' the Duke replied loftily.

'I don't know what's the world a-coming to,'

Jenkins muttered beneath his breath. 'Your Grace going off alone, an' dressed in such a hobbledehoy fashion.'

The Duke did not reply, he merely filled his pockets with the money that Mr Dunham had brought upstairs to his bedroom.

As he did so, he could see in the looking-glass that Jenkins was rolling up the clothes he wished to take with him in a waterproof cover that could be attached to the back of the saddle.

The Valet then produced two black slippers, which could be inserted in the pockets of the saddle.

Then with a resigned expression in his voice, he left the bedroom to take them down the stairs.

The Duke looked round, and for a moment he regretted leaving the grand four-poster bed, with its red silk curtains and his insignia emblazoned in bright colours over the pillows.

He could see the velvet jewel-boxes containing his decorations, which if he had stayed in London he would have worn tonight at a Ball that was being given by the Duke and Duchess of Bedford, at their delightful house in Russell Square.

The Duchess was very attractive, but as the Duke thought of her he remembered that if he attended the Ball, as he had meant to do, Imogen would have been waiting for him.

She would have been looking exceedingly beautiful, for with her fair hair, big blue eyes and flawless complexion he had thought when he first saw her, that she was the very embodiment of loveliness and no man could ask for more.

He was certain, now he thought about it, that Imogen did not desire him as ardently as her father and mother did.

She was, in fact, so stupid that the Duke thought it unlikely her desire for anything extended beyond the reflection of her own face in the mirror.

Lord Wentover was however well aware of his value as a son-in-law, while Lady Wentover must have deliberately enveigled other hostesses into helping her to secure a Ducal husband for Imogen.

Looking back the Duke remembered how at every dinner-party Imogen was always seated beside him.

At house-parties to which young girls were not usually invited Imogen had been there, and it was only because she was so beautiful that he had been seduced away from his liaison with a fascinating older woman, who was in fact, married to a Statesman of some repute.

Imogen, always Imogen!

He thought now he had fallen into the trap that had been set for him, as if he had been a greenhorn tasting the delights of London for the first time.

'How could I have been so foolish to think that for one moment she would content me as a wife,' he asked, 'or even be capable with her lack of brains of filling the role that would be required of her as Duchess of Brockenhurst?'

He remembered how house-parties at which his mother played Hostess at Hurst Castle, or any of his father's other houses, had always seemed to sparkle.

The male guests had been distinguished, intelligent and witty while beautiful, elegant and sophisticated women had added to the entertainment.

As a young man, the Duke could remember more clearly than anything else the interesting topics that were discussed around the dinner-table, when the ladies had retired to the Drawing Room.

Or after hunting the men would gather in the Library of the Castle, to talk of the Castle, to talk of the run of the day, the political situation and, of course, the news of the War.

'Damn it!' the Duke said to himself, 'I have not only got soft in the body but in the brain.'

It made him so angry that he spurred Samson into a gallop, and it was only when both master and horse were breathless, that the Duke drew in the reins so that they went at a more moderate speed.

He was so deep in thought that it was only when the sun sank in a blaze of glory over the horizon, and the first evening star was visible in the translucent sky, that the Duke realised he must find somewhere to stay the night.

He had ridden across country, and he had an idea that he was considerably further North than he might have expected.

Now he returned to what he thought must be the main road, to look for an Inn.

Two miles later he found one, and thought vaguely he remembered passing it on a previous journey, but he had never stayed there.

It appeared from the outside as if it might be comfortable within.

On closer inspection he appreciated there were quite good stables off the large courtyard, in which there was a prosperous-looking travelling chariot.

The Duke made up his mind that both he and Samson had gone far enough and he would stay the night there. At the same time remembering the conditions of Freddie's wager, he knew he must be careful that the chariot did not belong to anyone he knew.

He found an Ostler, inspected the Stable in which Samson was to be housed, and saw there were a number of other horses in adjacent stalls.

'I see you are busy tonight!' he remarked.

'Aye, Sir,' the Ostler replied. 'A party arrived two hours ago. 'Tis lucky, for we b'aint had many visitors lately.'

'Do you know the name of these people?' the Duke enquired.

The Ostler shook his head and the Duke walked into the Inn.

The Proprietor was a large, fat man. He was giving orders to two young girls in mobcaps, who the Duke suspected were serving in the Dining Hall.

The Proprietor turned as the Duke entered and recognised him as being a gentleman and a customer. He immediately began bowing subserviently.

' 'Evening, Sir, what can I do for ye, Sir? Is it dinner ye be wanting, or a bed for th' night?'

'I want a bed for the night,' the Duke replied, 'and I have already put my horse into the

Stables.'

The proprietor scratched his head.

'Our best rooms be already occupied, Sir. But there be 'un on th' first floor which be comfortable, if not over-large.'

'That will suit me,' the Duke said. 'I will also be wanting dinner. I presume you have a private parlour?'

'There be only one, Sir, an' that be already bespoke. But we'll make ye comfortable in th' Dining Hall.'

The Duke had learned what he wanted—that the people who occupied the travelling-chariot were dining in their own private parlour and were not likely to see him.

'Show me the bedroom,' he ordered. 'I would like dinner as soon as I have washed.'

His air of authority was obviously impressive, and the Landlord instead of sending one of the chambermaids showed him to the first floor.

The bedroom the Duke saw, was in fact, very small, and he realised it was the Dressing Room of an adjoining room with a communicating door with two bolts to secure it.

The Duke noted the place was clean.

'Would ye like some hot water, Sir,' the Landlord enquired.

'Thank you,' the Duke answered.

It took a little time to be brought upstairs, and while he was waiting the Duke wondered if he should fetch his clothes from the back of Samson's saddle, or wait until after he had eaten.

He decided on the latter course. Then when the water arrived he washed the dust from his face and hands, dried himself on a coarse towel and after a glance in the mirror to see that his cravat was tidy, went downstairs.

There were only two other people in the Dining Hall, which was a pleasant, oak-beamed room. The Duke sized them up as being superior servants.

He guessed that even in such a small Inn the coachmen and outriders, if there were any, would eat in the kitchen.

To his surprise he was positively hungry—something he did not remember having been for a long time. So he did full justice to a well-cooked steak, kidney and lark pie, and ate three slices of the home-cured ham.

Thinking that the wine was likely to be inferior, he drank what the Landlord informed him was home-brewed cider.

As he finished his meal with cheese and bread which undoubtedly had been baked that morning, he thought with a smile that Freddie would approve the much more spartan meal than he usually ate.

At the same time he could hardly say that he had met, today at any rate, any 'real people' who he had been told were so important to his journey.

He could not believe that he would find the conversation of the servants at the other table at all stimulating. He was certain the vocabulary of the Landlord was very limited.

'The sooner this journey is over the better,' he told himself. 'I am going to bed early and getting up early. When Freddie loses his Canaletto it will teach him a sharp lesson.'

As soon as the Duke had finished dinner, he went to the Stables to collect his clothes from the back of the saddle and to see if Samson was comfortable.

The great stallion pricked up his ears at his approach and nuzzled him when he patted his neck.

'If we have to go York, Samson,' the Duke said, 'we might even do it in record time and then return to our home comforts. What do you think?'

The horse appeared to be listening to him, then blew through his nostrils.

'I agree with you,' the Duke said. 'The whole

idea is damned nonsense from start to finish.'

He picked up the rainproof roll, put it over his arm and walked back to the Inn.

CHAPTER 2

The Duke opened wide the casement in his bedroom, and stood for a long time looking out onto the night. He was thinking about himself, and what Freddie had said to him.

He did not feel tired, and wondered if he should go downstairs and take a walk outside. Then he thought if he did so he might encounter the party who were occupying the private parlour. It would be wiser to stay where he was.

Two candles were the only light in his room, but they were enough to enable him to read the local paper, which he had picked up in the Hall before he came upstairs.

It was full of prizes that had been won at a local Show and did not concern itself with politics.

The Duke turned over the pages, saw there was nothing to interest him and decided he would undress.

He had taken off his riding-coat, and was just going to remove his boots when he heard a voice speaking so loudly and so clearly that for a moment it made him start.

Then he realised that someone was in the next room, with which his communicated.

'I want to make it quite clear to you, Valora,' a woman said, 'that when you arrive tomorrow you will make yourself pleasant to Sir Mortimer.'

'I have told you already, Stepmama,' another voice answered, 'that I will not marry Sir Mortimer, and I shall tell him so.'

'You will marry him if I have to beat you into submission, as undoubtedly he will do once you are his wife.'

There was a little scream of protest from the younger voice, that of the girl who had been addressed as Valora.

'How can you say such a thing?' she asked. 'How can you threaten me? If Papa was alive he would be horrified at the way you are behaving.'

'Your father is dead,' her Stepmother said almost brutally. 'Get it into your head that I am now your Guardian, and you will marry whom I want you to marry, if I take you to the altar unconscious.'

There was a pause for a moment. Then Valora said:

'I have tried to think why you should have chosen Sir Mortimer as my husband, but now I am almost sure it is because he has paid you. You spent all Papa's money, and you want more.'

'I have a good mind to slap you for your impertinence,' her Stepmother replied. 'But instead I will tell you that Sir Mortimer values you so highly, though God knows why, that the day you become his wife I shall receive a cheque for £10,000. In my opinion it is a good deal more than you are worth.'

'So you are selling me as if I were a piece of merchandise,' Valora answered bitterly. 'Well, you will be disappointed! I think Sir Mortimer, rich though he may be, is a horrible, disgusting debauched old man. I would rather die than become his wife.'

'Die then!' her Stepmother replied lightly. 'But oblige me by waiting until you have his ring on your finger.'

There was a sound as if Valora stamped her foot before she said:

'I will not do it! Let me try to make you understand that I will not be married in such a horrible and immoral manner.'

'If you think that is immoral,' her Stepmother remarked, 'then all I can say is you are fortunate that he offers you marriage. I daresay he would pay the same if you occupied a very different position in his life.'

There was a little murmur of protest, but Valora did not reply, and after a moment her Stepmother said:

'I have threatened you with the whip, and I shall not hesitate to use it if you make any sort of scene when we arrive at Heverington Hall. What is more, you need make no effort to try and escape before we get there.'

She waited as if she expected Valora to say something, but when she was still silent she continued:

'I am not a fool. I am well aware of why you gave instructions to the grooms to put your horse in the paddock tonight rather than the Stable. I intend to lock you in this room, and unless you are prepared to break your leg by jumping out of the window, you will be here waiting for me in the morning.'

'Morning or night, tomorrow or the next day, I will still not marry Sir Mortimer.'

As Valora finished speaking there was the sound of a hard stinging slap against soft flesh and a shrill cry of pain.

'You will marry him,' her Stepmother said, and there was a note of grim determination in her voice that was menacing.

Then the Duke heard footsteps walking across the room, a heavy door being shut and a key turned in the lock.

There was silence until he thought he heard the sound of a bed creak as if Valora had thrown herself down on it, followed by the sound of weeping.

He realised he had been standing still, listening to what was going on in the next door room, and was undisguisedly curious about the scene he had just overheard.

When the Stepmother had mentioned Heverington Hall he had realised he knew, almost with a sense of shock, the man they were talking about.

He had seen Sir Mortimer Heverington at various race-meetings, and he was in fact a member of White's Club, though the Duke had not met him there.

A large man of about fifty years of age, he was someone with whom the Duke had no wish to become acquainted for he knew that Sir Mortimer had an extremely unsavoury reptuation.

He was a racehorse owner about whom there were a number of stories concerning the way he ran his horses, which were not to his credit.

He was also a bad loser at cards, and the

Duke remembered vaguely in the back of his mind that Freddie had made some very derogatory comments about Sir Mortimer's taste in women.

The Duke was aware that there were certain establishments in London, patronised by gentlemen he would not number among his friends, who had a preference for abnormal erotic practices.

The more reputable, if that was the right word, Houses of Pleasure would not sink to providing anything so unnatural and the Duke despised those who found that sort of thing pleasurable.

Now at the back of his mind he was sure that he had heard that Heverington was the sort of man who enjoyed seducing very young girls and treating them sadistically.

He was sure that that was what Valora's Stepmother meant when she spoke of her being beaten by ber husband, and he felt revolted by the idea and at the same time very angry.

If there was one thing the Duke detested it was cruelty of any sort.

He was ruthless in dismissing any groom who neglected his horses. He had once personally thrashed one of his keepers for ill-treating a dog, and had dismissed him from his employment without notice.

The idea that Valora, whoever she might be, should be subjected to the brutal treatment that Heverington and his like found entertaining made him decide that he must do something to prevent it.

He could hear Valora sobbing and, as the sound was slightly muffled, he thought she must be crying into her pillow.

Without really thinking, he walked towards the bolted door which communicated with the adjoining bedroom, and only as he reached it did he tell himself he should not interfere.

Whatever happened to this girl it was none of his business.

It was only by sheer chance he had overheard what had been said, and if he were as usual at his house in Berkeley Square and actually at this moment dancing at the Duchess of Richmond's Ball, she would have had to sort out her own problems.

Then he heard the heartfelt sobs coming from the next room, and he knew that whatever the consequences to himself he could not "pass by on the other side".

"Nor would I be able to sleep," he told his conscience defensively, and knocked on the door.

Because he had made a very light knock, there was no immediate reaction, except he thought the sobs ceased and Valora was perhaps listening.

He knocked again.

Then a low, frightened little voice asked: 'Who is...it?'

'Come to the door in the wall,' the Duke said very softly.

He thought for a moment she was too surprised to believe what she was hearing. Then he heard the movement of her raising herself from the bed and her footsteps on the floor.

'Who are you?' she asked.

'Someone who is ready to help you escape, if that is what you want,' the Duke replied.

He thought that he heard her draw in her breath and went on:

'Have you a bolt on your side of the door?'

'There are two.'

'I have the same. If you think I can assist you, draw them back.'

There was a little pause, and the Duke thought she was wondering if she could trust him.

Then quickly as if she acted impulsively, he heard her pull back the bolt at the top of the door, and then the one at the bottom.

He did the same, and now it was easy to open the door into her room. He was facing Valora.

He had expected, after what he had overheard, for her to be young and attractive, but not quite so small or so lovely.

Although she had been crying and the tears were still on her cheeks and her long eyelashes wet, she had a flower-like innocent face of a very young child.

It struck the Duke, and he hated the thought as it came into his mind, that she was just the sort of helpless creature a man who was brutal and sadistic would enjoy torturing.

Then he realised Valora was looking at him questioningly and because he wished to reassure her, he smiled.

The Duke's smile on his extremely attractive face was something that women had found beguiling since he had first used it to his advantage while he was still in the cradle, when he wanted to get his own way.

'You must have...overheard what my...Stepmother said...to me,' Valora said in a hestitating little voice.

'It was unavoidable,' the Duke replied. 'The walls are thin, and this door does not fit very well.'

'Then you...understand I...have to run...away.'

'I gathered that was in your mind,' the Duke said.

As she still stood in the doorway facing him he went on:

'If you would like to talk about it to me I suggest you come in, and we close this door in case we are overheard.'

Valora shuddered, looking over her shoulder almost as if she expected to see her Stepmother entering the room from the other door which she had locked.

She obeyed the Duke, passing him, and he closed the door behind her.

When he turned to look at her she was standing helplessly in a small space between the bed and the window, looking at him with eyes that seemed to fill her whole face.

'I am afraid we are somewhat limited as to choice,' the Duke said in a calm voice. 'You sit on the bed and I will sit on the only chair. I hope it will not collapse under my weight.'

Valora gave a little faint sound, which might have been a laugh, and sat down on the side of the bed as he had suggested.

The Duke brought the hard wicker-seated chair nearer to her and sat down gingerly.

'Now,' he said, 'suppose we try and make some plans as to what you can do. I gather you have no wish to be married.'

His words made Valora stiffen and he saw her clench her thin fingers into the palm of her hand.

'I cannot...marry him,' she replied in a tense little voice. 'He is...horrible...and very old.'

'I agree that he is a most unsuitable husband for any woman, let alone someone as young as you are,' the Duke said sharply.

'You know Sir Mortimer Heverington?'

'I have heard of him,' the Duke answered cautiously.

'The moment I saw him I knew that he...repelled and...disgusted me,' Valora said, 'but I never...imagined that he would wish to...marry me.'

She looked so lovely with the light from the candles illuminating her fair hair, and revealing the whiteness of her skin against her simple evening gown that the Duke could understand only too well that Sir Mortimer had found her desirable.

But because he did not wish to think about it, he asked:

'If you escape, where would you go?'

'I have...thought about that for a...long time,' Valora replied. 'After Papa died Stepmama rented a house in London far too soon for propriety. She said she intended to marry me off as quickly as possible, but really I think she hoped to find another husband for herself.'

Valora's eyes were very large as she said in a horrified tone:

'When Sir Mortimer first...came to the house I thought he was...courting her not...me.'

'Surely there were other men who might have offered for you?'

'I do not...think Stepmama knew many... people,' Valora replied hesitantly. 'We were not...asked to any of the Grand Balls, and very few people...called on us.'

'Why was that?' the Duke enquired.

Valora did not look at him, as she said somewhat uncomfortably:

'I think the...hostesses in London did not... approve of Stepmama, just as Papa's... friends in the country did not...call on her.'

'Why not?'

Valora did not answer. Then after a moment he said:

'If I have to help you it is best if I know the truth about you. As it is I do not even know your name except I overheard you being called Valora.'

'My father,' Valora replied, 'was Lord Melford.'

She spoke as if she was sure it would mean something to the Duke and for a moment he thought he must ask for details, then he remembered.

There had been a tremendous scandal two or three years ago when Lord Melford had run away with the wife of a well-known actor.

It had been a case in which he had been sued for seduction, which had the gossips licking their lips at the revelations which filled the less respectable newspapers and delighted the cartoonists.

Finally there was talk of a divorce, which would have to be taken to the House of Lords. However the actor had had a sudden heart attack during a performance at the Theatre Royal, Drury Lane, and died before a doctor could be fetched.

It had all been extremely dramatic, and had taken up a great deal of newsprint.

At first there had even been speculation as to whether Lord Melford had been party to murdering his paramour's revengeful husband.

Death, however, was proved to be from natural causes, and the Duke had heard in the Club that Melford had been fool enough to marry his mistress, who naturally was not likely to be accepted socially.

Almost as if she knew the thoughts that were passing through the Duke's mind, Valora said:

'Now, I...think you...understand!'

'I do!' the Duke replied, 'and I am very sorry for you.'

'I am only...sorry for...myself,' Valora answered, 'because my Stepmother wishes me to...marry. If I had the choice it is something that I have no intention of doing.'

The Duke looked puzzled.

'You mean you have no intention of marrying Hevertington?'

'Or anyone...else,' Valora said quickly.

'This is ridiculous,' the Duke expostulated. 'Of course you must marry. But as you are very young there is no hurry.'

'I am eighteen,' Valora said, 'and though you may think it strange, if I can live my own life I do not intend to marry anyone.'

'Why?' the Duke asked curiously.

'It would take some time to explain my feelings on this matter,' Valora replied. 'But now please help me to escape. I must be a long way from here before Stepmama realised I have gone.'

'I agree that is important,' the Duke answered, 'but at the same time where do you think of going?'

'My grandfather, Mama's father, lives in York,' Valora said. 'He is very old, but I think if I can reach him, he can prove to be my proper Guardian rather than Stepmama.'

The Duke thought this was intelligent thinking.

'I am sure he will,' he said, 'and by an extraordinary coincidence I am on my way to York.'

He thought there was a sudden light in Valora's eyes before she said:

'I would not...wish to trouble you...if you could allow me to leave through your room once everyone is asleep in the Inn, I can find Mercury and be on my way.'

'I thought it clever of you to suggest he should be in the paddock rather than the Stable,' the Duke remarked.

'I will have to ride him without a saddle,' Valora said. 'Perhaps if I have enough money I will be able to buy one, once I am well ahead of those who will try and catch me.'

'Are you suggesting that your Stepmother will send the servants after you?'

'Of course she will,' Valora answered. 'She has her special factotum with her, a man called Walter. He is a horrible creature who spies on people, and he has been running the household ever since Papa died.'

The Duke thought that he was probably one of the men who had been eating in the Dining Hall.

'I expect too,' Valora went on, 'she would send Giles who works with Walter and perhaps one of the outriders.'

She gave a little shiver that seemed to shake her whole body, as she said:

'She will do everything in her power to prevent me escaping. She wants the £10,000 that Sir Mortimer has promised her, and will fight desperately not to lose it.'

'I see we shall have to be clever if we are to circumvent her plans,' the Duke replied reflectively.

'I do not want to be a...nuisance or an...encumbrance to...you,' Valora said.

'I have a feeling you might get into far worse trouble if you travel alone,' the Duke answered.

'Nothing could be worse than having to marry Sir Mortimer,' Valora replied fervently.

The Duke was sure she had no idea of the dangers that she could encounter riding in the countryside.

Even as he thought that she should go with him, he knew it would be extremely stupid of him to get involved with someone like Lady Melford and an outsider like Sir Mortimer.

He was sensible enough to realise that it would obviously be very much in their interest to blackmail him for abducting a minor and rather than face a sentence of transportation he would have to meet their demands however exorbitant.

Common sense told him that in his position he should let Valora make the journey to York alone, and disassociate himself both from her and the people with whom he was involved.

Then he thought again of Sir Mortimer's sadistic streak, and as he looked at the small frail figure silhouetted against the candlelight and the child-like face turned towards him, he knew he could not abandon her.

He began to plan what they would do, almost as if he was back in the War, thinking how he could get his men into a strategic position, yet out of range of the enemy.

Then he realised that Valora was waiting, her large eyes fixed on his face, he said:

'I think the wisest thing would be for you to have some sleep. We shall have to ride hard as soon as it is light, and the worst thing would be for you to collapse from exhaustion.'

'I shall not do that,' Valora replied. 'Could we not go now?'

'I think that would be a mistake,' the Duke

said. 'The Proprietor would think it strange that I should leave before enjoying the somewhat doubtful comfort of his bed. And if there was the slightest suspicion that you were leaving with me, he would undoubtedly alert one of your servants who would waken your Stepmother.'

Valora clasped her fingers together.

'You are right...of course you are right, and very wise. As you say, we must...think this out very...carefully.'

She drew in her breath before she added:

'If I fail to escape now...tomorrow night I shall be at...Heverington Hall.'

'Then do what I tell you,' the Duke said. 'Go to your bedroom and try to sleep. I will wake you at four o'clock, which is about the time dawn breaks.'

Valora rose from the bed, then as the Duke rose too she stood looking up at him.

'I am sure it is...wrong of me to involve you in my troubles and...difficulties,' she said, 'but I am very grateful.'

'I am honoured you should trust me.'

She smiled. It was the first time she had done so, and it made her look very lovely.

'I knew I could do that the moment I saw you.'

'Thank you.'

Valora started to move to the communicating door, and as she reached it he said:

'You realise you can bring with you only what can be attached to the back of your saddle, if we can find one for you.'

'I had already thought of that,' Valora answered, 'and actually I had my things ready before I went down to dinner.'

'Then try to sleep,' the Duke said.

She smiled at him again, went into her own room and shut the door behind her.

The Duke undressed and got into bed.

He had taught himself in the Army to wake at whatever time he wanted, and having registered in his mind that he must rise at four o'clock he shut his eyes and relaxed.

Once again he caught himself thinking that he was being very foolhardy in getting himself mixed up with Valora, her Stepmother, and worst of all—Heverington.

Then he remembered Freddie's instructions that he should meet real people, and wondered if this was what they were.

Even Valora with her child-like beauty seemed unreal. It was certainly strange that she had said she had no intention of being married.

'I shall ask her to explain that tomorrow,' he

thought.

But he knew the real question was whether they would be able to escape from the Inn.

★ ★ ★ ★

The Duke awoke with a start and saw the first faint light of dawn was coming through the uncurtained window.

He sat up to look at his watch that he had put beside him before he went to sleep. The hands pointed at ten minutes to the hour.

He got out of bed, washed in cold water, and when he was decently clothed in his shirt and breeches, he opened the communicating door between his room and Valora's.

He knew it would be unwise, as silence enveloped the Inn, to talk.

At this hour, the sound of a voice however slight would carry and perhaps wake those who were sleeping more lightly than they had earlier in the night.

As he expected, Valora was fast asleep.

He walked in his stockinged feet quietly towards the bed and he could see her eyelashes were dark against her cheeks. She looked very young and defenceless with her golden hair flowing over her shoulder and the pillow.

He stood looking at her for a moment before he put out his hand and very gently touched her shoulder.

She opened her eyes immediately and bemused with sleep and perhaps he thought, her dreams, she stared at him, as if she did not recognise him.

'It is nearly four o'clock,' he said in a whisper.

She made as if to sit up.

'Do not speak if you can help it, just get dressed and join me.'

Without waiting for a reply he left her and went back to his own room.

By the time he had pulled on his boots, tied his cravat in the manner which Jenkins found so lamentably old-fashioned, and packed his night-shirt and razor, Valora joined him.

She was wearing a dark blue riding-habit, which was very smartly cut, but fortunately was not a very distinctive colour, and on her head was a high-crowned hat draped with a gauze veil, which would certainly not have looked out of place in Rotten Row.

She was carrying a rolled-up bundle which the Duke knew contained the necessities she was bringing with her.

There was a look of excitement in her face combined with an expression of trust, which he thought reminded him of the spaniels which followed him everywhere when he was at the Castle.

'I have been thinking over what we should do,' he said in a low tone. 'I am going to go downstairs and see if there is anyone about. When I find the coast is clear I want you to follow me and go straight to the paddock to your horse.'

Valora nodded but she did not speak.

'I imagine he will be without a bridle, and I will collect one from the Stable with my own horse, and if it is possible find your saddle. If not we shall have to buy one.'

Again Valora nodded.

Without saying any more the Duke picked up the roll which contained his belongings, took a quick look round the bedroom to see he had not left anything behind, and opened the door.

The inside of the Inn was in darkness. There was deep silence, and no one appeared to be moving.

The Duke walked down the oak stairs on tip-toe, and when he reached the bottom he went to the door oppposite the Dining Hall, which he was sure was the way into the kitchen.

There was still no sound of movement or voices, and he beckoned to Valora who was standing in the doorway of his bedroom. She seemed to almost float down the stairs without making a sound.

He opened the door of the Inn. She slipped past him, and he saw her run across the courtyard.

The Duke then went to the counter on which the Proprietor kept his ledger. He put down on it two guineas, then walked in a normal manner from the Inn across the courtyard to the stables.

He expected that the servants and the outriders who had accompanied Lady Melford and Valora would be sleeping in the hay-attic, as was usual in wayside Inns. Walter would undoubtedly have a bed on the second floor, if there was one.

The Duke walked towards the stall where he had left Samson. He lifted down his bridle from a hook on the opposite wall and picked up his saddle which had been laid beneath it.

Samson made no difficulties about the Duke saddling him rather than a groom.

As he tightened the girth, the Duke saw a lady's saddle which he was sure was Valora's lying on the floor in the passageway beneath a bridle, as his had been.

He led Samson out of the Stable, and then

quickly lifted down Valora's bridle and put her saddle over his.

Even as he did so he heard the sound of a man yawning and then spitting overhead, and he knew that Samson's movements had awoken either one of the Ostlers or the Melford coachmen.

Hastily, because there was no time to be lost, he led Samson across the yard and round the side of the Stables.

As he suspected the paddock was a small and badly-fenced piece of grass, which was just behind the building.

At the gate Valora was standing with a bay horse nuzzling her, which the Duke recognised as a fine thoro'bred.

He took Samson up to her at a run, transferred her saddle on to Mercury's back and handed her the bridle.

At a speed which he felt could not have been bettered by any Sergeant-Major, the Duke had the girths fastened, and lifted Valora into the saddle before he mounted Samson.

Then they were off, riding at a speed that made the tufts of grass fly out behind the horses' hooves.

It was some moments before Valora exclaimed:

'We have done it!...we have done it!... How can I thank you? I could never have managed to get Mercury's saddle by myself.'

'We have a long way to go,' the Duke said solemnly. 'It is unlucky to assume we have won until we have reached York.'

Valora smiled at him, and for the first time he noticed she had a dimple on either side of her mouth.

'I have always believed the first step is the most difficult,' she replied, 'and we have taken that in style.'

She spoke with a lilt in her voice that the Duke had not heard before, and he replied:

'By all means let us be optimistic, but not foolhardy.'

'I have a feeling in my bones that we shall reach Grandpapa,' she said, 'and nothing you can say would depress me at this moment.'

Even as she spoke she looked over her shoulder apprehensively almost as if she felt they might have been pursued.

There was nothing to see except the soft ground mist which hid everything but the roof of the Inn from sight, and even that was gradually fading into the distance.

'Ride!' the Duke ordered tersely. 'And I only hope Mercury can keep up with Samson.'

'You insult him,' Valora replied indignantly.

At the same time she knew he was speaking sense. She pushed Mercury into a gallop, and she and the Duke moved side by side as the sun rose over the horizon.

They rode for nearly three hours across country, the Duke making no attempt to jump hedges but deliberately because it was less arduous, finding the gates or gaps and all the time avoiding the roads.

He was beginning to feel hungry, and though she did not complain, he was sure Valora felt the same.

Then he saw ahead of them a small village which appeared to consist merely of a small grey stone Norman Church and a few black and white thatched cottages.

For the first time for nearly an hour the Duke spoke.

'I think we have earned our breakfast,' he said, 'and I admit to feeling extremely hungry.'

'So am I,' Valora replied, 'but I thought you might consider it far from a necessary emotion at such a crucial moment.'

'I hope the moment is less crucial than it was,' the Duke answered dryly, 'and eggs and bacon seem to me just now as delectable as anything a superaltive Chef could devise.'

Even as he spoke he feared that to talk in such a manner might suggest he was a rich man.

He hoped Valora did not notice or reflect that the average gentleman who rode alone without a groom did not employ a Chef.

She made no comment. But the Duke told himself that from the way she behaved she was obviously quick-witted and perceptive, and unless he wished her to be suspicious about his identity he would have to be more careful what he said in the future.

He was not surprised, when they were seated outside a small Inn named *'The Dog and Duck'*, having ordered for breakfast everything that was available, that Valora said:

'You know my name, but you have not told me yours. I can hardly address you as "My Good Samaritan", which indeed is what you are.'

The Duke remembered that was what he had thought he was, when he could not "pass by on the other side". He considered quickly what he could call himself.

He had considered, when he had set out on the journey, taking Freddie's name.

Now he decided Valora might have heard of it since Freddie's father was a member of the Cabinet, and his Uncle was in the House of

Lords. He therfore altered it.

'My name is Standon,' he said, 'Greville Standon.'

He used one of his own Christian names which everyone had almost forgotten because his friends and his relatives all called him Brock.

'Greville Standon!' Valora repeated. 'It is a nice name and suits you.'

The Duke smiled.

'Just as Valora suits you. Have you any idea why it was chosen?'

'My mother was very well read,' Valora answered, 'and wanted to give me a name that was unusual. Papa was not interested as I was not a son.'

She smiled before she added:

'I was in fact a disappointment to him from the moment I was born. But sometimes he treated me as if I were a boy, and I enjoyed that.'

The Duke thought it was difficult to think of anyone who looked less masculine and more feminine than Valora, but he merely asked:

'What did you learn in that particular capacity?'

'I learned to shoot, and swim, and Papa did not object to paying teachers who taught me Latin and Greek.'

The Duke was surprised.

'Certainly the sort of education a boy receives.'

'That is what I enjoyed,' Valora answered. 'So you can quite understand why, apart from any other reason, I would never wish to marry someone like Sir Mortimer who has not an intelligent thought in his head.'

She spoke so scathingly the Duke laughed and she added:

'Most men I have met are the same. Their vocabulary is limited to a few hundred words, and they have no interests apart from hoping the horse on which they have put their money will come in first, and the cards they are holding in their hands will win the trick.'

The Duke laughed again.

'You certainly condemn us as a sex. I feel I should apologise for being a man.'

'It was certainly clever the way you obtained my saddle for me.'

'Thank you!' the Duke replied sarcastically.

As if she was afraid she had offended him, she said:

'Please, I am not being critical of you, I am very, very grateful for what you have done for me. It is only that as a general rule I find men stupid and unimaginative and very badly educated.'

'You have obviously met a large number of the species,' the Duke answered mockingly.

'I met a great many of Papa's friends,' Valora replied, 'and a number of men when I was in London with my Stepmother, but none of them altered the opinion I formed when Mama and I discussed it before she died.'

The Duke helped himself to several more eggs from the large dish which had been placed between them on the rough wooden table.

'I imagine your Mother's opinions were the same as yours.'

Valora gave a little sigh.

'I think Mama was frustrated and not very happy. You see she was never very strong after I was born and was obliged to rest a great deal, and she knew that it bored Papa who used to be away a lot.'

There was something in the way she spoke which made the Duke suspect she had an idea of what her Father did when he was away from home, but he merely said:

'So your Mother encouraged you to use your brain.'

'She said that knowledge was the one thing which would never disappoint me,' Valora said simply.

'Surely because you have a great deal of knowledge it does not make you hate men, and preclude you from marrying.'

'I suppose I might meet a Professor whom I might find very interesting,' Valora replied speculatively, 'but I doubt if in these circumstances he would want to marry me.'

'You are full of surprises,' the Duke remarked. 'I have never met a young woman before who has made up her mind she would not marry because men were not clever enough for her. What do you intend to do with your life?'

'I want to work at something useful, and if possible to improve the standard of education for children.'

The Duke stared at her.

Without waiting for an answer, she went on:

'Surely you realise how disgraceful it is that the great majority of people in this country have no education at all. A few of the great Estates have schools for the children of their employees, but most employers do not want the working class to have brains, just hands with which they can labour.'

She spoke passionately, and the Duke found it difficult to know what he should reply.

He had an idea that there were schools on his Estate for small children, but he was not certain. If there were, he had certainly not visited them, nor had he any report on their progress.

He made a mental note that this was something he must enquire into when he got home.

Because at the moment he thought he was rather out of his depth, he helped himself to several slices of a quite edible ham that was standing on the table, and as he did so, he said:

'I am extremely interested in what you are saying, Valora, but we should not linger any longer than is strictly necessary. The further north we are before nightfall the safer.'

'Yes, of course.'

She hesitated a moment and went on:

'I am sorry if I am boring you with the subject that interests me. It is a very long time since I have been able to talk about it to anyone.'

'I am interested,' the Duke said firmly, 'and perhaps tonight over dinner, when there is no hurry, I shall be able to sharpen up my brains so as to argue with you on equal terms.'

He spoke a little cynically, thinking it was an impertinence of any young girl to think she knew more than he did.

But he saw that Valora was looking at him

excitedly.

'I do hope you will do that,' she cried. 'It is something I will look forward to, more than I can possibly tell you.'

CHAPTER 3

The Duke drew in Samson and waited until Valora came to his side.

They had been riding through the woods in single file, and now the Duke found they were on high ground overlooking a valley.

He could see several small hamlets ranging away into the distance and was wondering whether it would be safe to stay in one or other of them.

He thought this afternoon when they passed two or three large houses that it would be a mistake to stay on some nobleman's Estate, who might either make enquiries as to who they were, or worse still, inform Lady Melford's servants that they had been seen.

It was growing late and the horses were tired, and he thought Valora must be too.

When he considered it he realised she was exceptional in that all the time they had been travelling she had never complained or in any way drawn attention to herself.

He could not imagine this happening with

any of the women he had known before. Always they were demanding his attention, if not flirtatiously then by trying to arouse his sympathy or his consideration.

Because they had been travelling fast conversation had been sparse, and when they did talk it had either been about their route or something that Valora found amusing or interesting by the wayside.

They had seen a man in the stocks, which at first had evoked her compassion, and then when they both realised he was too drunk to know where he was, it had seemed amusing.

The Duke knew too that Valora had been thrilled by the wild life they had seen in the woods.

It had been a slower way of travelling, but he had been wise enough to realise that in country districts two people on outstandingly fine horses, galloping on private land were bound to command attention.

Valora looked over the valley, as he did, and then she asked.

'Will it be wise to stay at an Inn? Perhaps we should sleep in the open.'

'It is not the type of restful night I enjoy,' the Duke replied dryly, 'Nor would I commend it as comfortable for you.'

'I am not afraid of discomfort,' Valora replied and added: 'In a good cause.'

'I think we will risk it.'

As he spoke he would have moved his horse forward, but a voice behind them said harshly:

'Stand and deliver!'

The Duke was astonished.

Then he turned round to see that just behind them there was a man with a handkerchief over the lower part of his face, on a horse.

He realised he had been a fool, for not only would it be impossible for him to draw the pistol from his pocket without being shot in the process, but he was vividly aware that the money he carried was not concealed.

Too late he thought that on such a journey he should have placed the notes in the lining of his coat and distributed his sovereigns in more than one pocket.

Even as he thought of these things he was aware the pistol was pointed at his heart, and he began very slowly to raise his left hand.

Then the Highwayman gave an exclamation, and the Duke was aware he was not looking at him, but at Valora.

Suddenly the man pulled the handkerchief from his face and exclaimed:

'Miss Valora, what are you doing here?'

Valora had been looking over her shoulder as the Duke had been, at the intruder. Now she gave a cry of unmistakable delight and turned Mercury round.

'Mr Travers, is it really you?'

'It is indeed, Miss Valora,' the Highwayman replied, 'and what are you doing here and who is this man? Is he...'

'No...no,' Valora interrupted, 'he is a friend. He is helping me to escape from my Stepmother.'

Astonished at this exchange, the Duke looked at the Highwayman and saw that he was a man between thirty and forty, with a lean, sharp-boned face which, without his concealing handkerchief looked mild and unintimidating.

The Highwayman put his pistol into a holster on the front of his saddle before he said to Valora:

'So you have run away? I suspected that was what you would wish to do when I heard of your intended marriage.'

'You heard of it?'

'News travels quickly in the places I frequent,' the Highwayman said with a smile, 'and actually I was in the village of Heverington when I heard you were expected.'

'I escaped this morning,' Valora replied, 'thanks entirely to the help I received from Mr Standon.'

She indicated the Duke as she spoke. The Highwayman rode up to him and held out his hand.

'My name is Travers,' he said, 'and I am pleased to meet you. I had been thinking how I could help Miss Valora but I was afraid it would be impossible.'

'Oh, Mr Travers, you understand I could not marry a man like Sir Mortimer,' Valora cried.

'Of course not, and I would have prevented it even if I had to shoot Sir Mortimer first. If any man deserves to die, it is he.'

The way the Highwayman spoke made it more impressive because he did not raise his voice.

'How far are we away from Heverington now?' the Duke asked.

'About three miles.'

Valora gave a little cry of horror.

'Then we must ride further on. Suppose he hears that I am here in the vicinity.'

The Highwayman was silent for a moment, then he said:

'If you escaped this morning, then Sir Mortimer is not likely to be aware that you are missing until Her Ladyship reaches the Hall.'

'No, that is true,' Valora said, 'but surely it is dangerous to stay on his Estate?'

'There is not many on his land would tell him anything he wished to know,' the Highwayman said grimly.

The Duke interrupted to say:

'You will appreciate we have ridden a long way, and the horses are tired. Do you know of somewhere safe? We can leave again tomorrow morning at dawn.'

'I know just the place,' the Highwayman replied, 'where Miss Valora would be very much safer than she would be at Heverington Hall.'

He looked down at the valley and pointed to a small hamlet about a mile and half away.

'If you go down the hill for about a hundred yards,' he said, 'you will find a cart-track which will take you through the trees, onto a country lane on the other side of the wood. Follow it and you will come to the village. Look for *"The Magpie"*. It is an Inn on the green.'

'You do not think they will be...suspicious of...us?' Valora said in a frightened little voice.

'Coming along the road you will seem like ordinary travellers,' the Highwayman said, 'but I will go ahead and warn them of your approach.'

The Duke must have looked at him enquiringly, because the Highwayman grinned and said:

'They know me there, so I can personally recommend it!'

'Thank you, Mr Traves,' Valora exclaimed, 'and I am so happy to see you again!'

'As I to see you, Miss Valora. I have been worrying about you this past month, but I had no idea how I could get in touch with you.'

'Fate has been on our side,' Valora said lightly.

'Let us hope so,' the Highwayman answered quietly.

He lifted the reins of his horse.

'I will be getting on and please remember that I am not known by my real name in these parts, just as Bill.'

'We will remember,' Valora answered.

The Highwayman would have ridden off, but the Duke stopped him.

'One moment,' he said. 'I think it would be wiser if you say at the Inn we are brother and sister.'

'Of course!' the Highwayman exclaimed. 'Stupid of me not to think of it. What name will it be?'

The Duke tried to think if he had mentioned

his name the previous night at the Inn. Then he remembered that the Landlord had not asked him for one, and it was only when he was talking to Valora at breakfast that he had decided to call himself Standon.

'Standon is not a name,' he remarked, 'which will arouse much comment.'

'Your appearance will do that,' the Highwayman smiled. 'Do not worry; there is no one to see you except a few yokels.'

He spurred his horse and rode away through the trees, and only when he was out of sight did the Duke say:

'That was certainly a surprise, and it has taught me a lesson which I shall not forget.'

'What is that?' Valora asked.

'That not only should I be on my guard against Gentlemen of the Road, but also I must carry my money where I should not have to hand it over to the first fellow who asks for it at gunpoint.'

'I suppose I should say the same about my **jewellery**.'

'You have some with you?'

'All I possess I have pinned into my blouse under my jacket. I thought perhaps a Highwayman would not expect to find it there.'

The Duke had the idea that Highwaymen,

whom he had never encountered before as he always travelled well protected, would expect people to hide their valuables. If it suited them they would not hesitate to strip their victim.

'I will certainly take more care in future,' he said more sharply. 'I consider we both had a very lucky escape.'

Because he was angry with himself for having been caught unawares, he started to ride down the grassy incline towards the cart-track.

It was only when they had reached the country lane which the Highwayman had described to them, that Valora said:-

'I was so glad to see Mr Travers again, or rather Bill as he has told us to call him.'

'Who is he?' the Duke asked, 'and surely he is a very odd friend for you to have.'

'I thought you might think that,' Valora smiled. 'Actually he was my Latin teacher.'

The Duke looked at her in utter surprise.

He had been aware that the Highwayman spoke in an educated voice and he had in fact been so astonished by the whole encounter that he was now exceedingly curious.

'Tell me about him,' he said.

'Mr Travers was the Agent for the next Estate to ours,' Valora said. 'It belonged to Lord Mount who was old and noted for lording it over his Estate in an autocratic manner that even Papa said was out of date.'

The Duke wondered what Valora meant by this, but he did not interrupt as she went on:

'Mr Travers had read for the Bar and intended to practise as a Barrister, but although he did brilliantly at his University, he could not afford to wait to become established in a practice and when he got married he took the job with Lord Mount.'

'I should not have thought a Barrister was likely to make a good Agent,' the Duke remarked.

'I think Mr Travers was so clever he could have done anything well, and as he was brought up in the country he understood how an Estate should be run. It was more than that horrible old Lord Mount did.'

'What happened?' the Duke asked.

'Lord Mount discovered that Mr Travers was teahing the children of the labourers to read and write. There was no kind of schooling available for them, and because he thought this was wrong Mr Travers gave them lessons in his free time on Sundays.'

Valora's voice deepend with anger as she went on:

'Lord Mount discovered this and accused Mr

Travers of teaching the people he employed to be revolutionaries. So he dismissed him and turned him out of his house without notice.'

'I can hardly believe it!' the Duke exclaimed. 'Surely there must have been other reasons.'

'No! Lord Mount loathed and feared any form of progress and what he described as "new fangled ideas".'

'It seems incredible,' the Duke murmured.

Even as he spoke he was aware there were quite a number of landlords who had no wish for their labourers to "better" themselves, or get what was called "ideas above their station".

'Mrs Travers was having a baby,' Valora said in a low voice. 'She was not only upset about what had happened to her husband, but they had to travel a long distance to her parents' home, and she...died.'

There was a sob in Valora's voice as she said the last word.

'So Travers took to the road,' the Duke said.

'I believe the first person he robbed was Lord Mount,' Valora answered in a different tone. 'Though he has never talked about it to me, I feel sure it was not the money he took which pleased him but the feeling that for once in his life he had His Lordship at his mercy.'

The Duke laughed.

'One does not always get the chance of revenge so neatly. It was also a dangerous thing to do.'

'Very dangerous,' Valora agreed. 'And of course now there is a price on his head. Papa was away when he was dismissed, and when he returned I begged him to do something to help Mr Travers. But by then it was too late. Lord Mount had notified the Magistrates and the Military were told to arrest him.'

'Which would mean he would be hanged on a gibbet at the crossroads,' the Duke said.

'I do not think he would mind very much,' Valora replied. 'He loved his wife, who was a very sweet person and he misses her badly.'

The Duke did not reply, for at that moment he saw ahead of them the village green.

There was the Inn they expected but very much smaller and more dilapidated than the one at which they had breakfasted, or another where they had stopped for bread and cheese later in the day.

Just for a moment the Duke thought it did not look a proper place for Valora, then he remembered they could not be particular. It certainly would be unwise to linger in the vicinity of Heverington Hall.

He thought Valora must be thinking the same

as he was.

She did not speak but he thought her eyes looked a little apprehensive as they drew nearer to the Inn.

Before they reached the front of it a small boy beckoned them, then scampered ahead as they followed him round the back of the building.

There was a Stable, obviously in bad repair with holes in the roof, attached to the Inn.

As the Duke dismounted, the Highwayman appeared at the back door to help Valora from the saddle. Then he drew nearer to the Duke to say in a low voice:

'I have changed your story. There would be no reason for you as a brother and sister to be secretive about yourselves.'

'Then what are we supposed to be?' the Duke asked.

'I said you were eloping to Gretna Green, and you were terrified you were being followed by the lady's parents who had forbidden the marriage.'

The Duke smiled.

'I see you have a fertile imagination.'

'Without one I should not last long,' the Highwayman replied. 'But all the world loves a lover, and they will hide you the best they can.'

'Thank you,' the Duke answered.

Valora's eyes were sparkling as she said:

'You are making this as exciting as one of the stories you used to tell me, and then make me translate it into Latin.'

'I miss those lessons,' the Highwayman replied, 'and most of all with the life I live now I miss books and intelligent people to talk to.'

He did not wait for an answer, but led Mercury by the bridle towards the tumbledown Stable.

The Duke followed but Valora hesitated.

An elderly woman, poorly dressed but nevertheless clean and tidy, appeared at the doorway of the Inn to say:

'Come in, dearie. Bill tells me ye've come a long way an' have a long way t'go. We'll have a comfortable bed for ye, an' we'll do our best t'find ye and yer man somethin' to fill yer bellies.'

'Thank you,' Valora said, and went into the Inn.

It was small and dark, with ceilings of heavy ship's beams, but the bedrooms were clean and the Landlady showed her proudly that the mattresses were filled with the best goose feathers.

'Ye'll sleep sound wi' naught t'worry ye,' she said.

Valora hoped it was true.

The Duke brought her bundle from the back of her saddle and she found that he was in a room which was even smaller than hers but still had a comfortable bed.

The Duke put the roll from his saddle on the floor and went downstairs.

On leaving the Stable he said to the Highwayman:

'I feel it would be inhospitable if I did not ask you to dine with us.'

'I would like to,' was the reply, 'but I think it would be a mistake. There is always a chance that some busybody might recognise me and at the moment I am thinking only of Miss Valora's safety.'

'I understand what you are saying,' the Duke replied, 'and I consider it very generous of you.'

'What I intend to do,' the Highwayman went on, 'is to go back to Heverington Hall to find out of Lady Melford has arrived without the bride, or whether she is putting off the evil hour of tell Sir Mortimer she is missing.'

'I hope it annoys him,' the Duke said grimly.

'It will,' the Highwayman replied. 'Whatever happens, you must prevent her from becoming the wife of a man who is so despicable that no decent woman should even speak to him.'

'I have heard some unpleasant things about him.'

'Unpleasant!' the Highwayman ejaculated. 'I would not soil my lips by describing the way he has behaved to local girls or the debaucheries of parties he has given at the Hall.'

He paused before he added:

'I am not exaggerating when I say I would have killed him rather than let him marry Miss Valora.'

'I can only say I admire you for your feelings, the Duke said.

'She is a very exceptional person,' the Highwayman went on. 'With her brains it is a pity she was not born a man, but no one except that avaricious strumpet who became her Stepmother would have thought of marrying her to someone like Sir Mortimer.'

'She is a bad woman?' the Duke asked.

'Beautiful and rotten to the core,' the Highwayman answered. 'I knew when Lord Melford married her there would be trouble but shortly after he brought her from London to his home, I had to leave mine, so I was unable to see Miss Valora or help her.'

'Yet you kept in touch with what was happening,' the Duke remarked.

'There were plenty of people to tell me what

was going on at Melford Manor because of my affection for as well as my admiration of the girl I taught for six years. I hoped she would find some decent man to marry her.'

'I understand after her mother died she was not likely to come in contact with what you call decent men.'

'That is true, a scandal is not forgotten easily in the country. And I suspect where London Society is concerned it is much the same.'

'That is what Valora told me,' the Duke replied.

'Where are you taking her now?'

It was a question which the Duke thought he might have expected, and there was a suspicion in the Highwayman's eyes that he thought he should resent, but at the same time he respected.

'I am taking her to her Grandfather who I understand lives in York.'

The Highwayman gave an exclamation of relief.

'I thought I could trust you.'

Again to the Duke's surprise he did not resent the frankness behind the words.

'I only hope I can get there safely,' he remarked.

'You must be careful of a man called Walter,'

the Highwayman said. 'He is a nasty bit of work. Her Ladyship employs him in a dozen different ways, and all of them unsavoury.'

'Valora has already spoken of him.'

'Giles, the man with him, is just as dangerous,' the Highwayman added.

They were talking outside the Inn door and the Duke said:

'As you are leaving I suggest you have a drink with me first.'

'I would rather not, but thank you all the same,' the Highwayman replied. 'I never drink when I am working.'

He smiled over the last word. Because in a way it was so outrageous the Duke smiled back. Then the Highwayman turned towards the Stable.

'I will see you in the morning,' he said. 'Tell Miss Valora from me there is no need to be afraid, nothing will happen tonight at any rate.'

He did not wait for a reply, and the Duke went into the Inn and up to his bedroom.

As he washed in the basin with the soap that Jenkins had packed for him, he thought he was certainly involved in a very strange adventure, which undoubtedly would evoke the approval of Freddie, if no one else.

How could he have imagined for one moment

he would rescue a girl from a sadist like Heverington, and encounter a Highwayman who was a teacher of Latin.

'No one would believe a word of it,' he thought to himself, and felt he strained even his own credulity in believing the events of the day.

Having tied a clean cravat round his neck, he knocked on the door next to his.

'Who is it?' Valora asked a little apprehensively.

'I am hungry,' the Duke replied.

'So am I,' she answered and opened the door.

The Duke was surprised. She had taken off her habit, and was wearing a very pretty gown of white silk.

Because he was extremely experienced where women's dress was concerned, he realised it was made of material that had not creased despite the fact it had been rolled up all day, and was also very simple.

It made her look very young and very fresh, and as she sensed his surprise, she smiled.

'I am afraid it is my whole wardrobe. If we take long in reaching York you will be extremely tired of seeing me in it.'

'You make me feel I should be taking you to a party,' the Duke said.

'I am quite content with the programme you have already devised,' Valora answered.

She walked ahead of him down the stairs, and the Landlord, a large fat rather loquacious man they had not met before, showed them into a small room which was obviously not often in use.

The one table it contained had been covered with a white cloth, and dinner appeared as soon as they were seated.

It was a simple meal and consisted of a soup that seemed to Valora because she was so hungry, delicious, followed by cold meats that the Duke guessed were kept for casual visitors, like Highwaymen, or more exclusively for the Proprietor himself.

The ham and the home-made brawn were quite palatable, especially when the pickles, that the Landlady assured them she made only this week, gave them a piquant taste.

There was cheese and a large plate of strawberries that had hastily been picked from the garden, to which they could add some thick cream, which they were told had been standing ready for the butter churning which was to take place tomorrow.

There was freshly-baked bread to eat with the meal, and once again the Duke preferred cider to the local beer or some dubious French wine.

'I have enjoyed every mouthful,' Valora said, as she finished the last strawberry.

The Duke thought of the huge meals that were served both in Berkeley Square or at the Castle for which he had often found he had no appetite.

There was no doubt that despite the exercise he took so arduously boxing in Gentleman Jackson's Acadamy in Bond Street, or fencing with *Signor* Balotti in his school at Hampstead, his body responded more naturally to a hard day's ride which had started at dawn and ended at sunset.

As they were both concentrating on their food they did not talk very much during the meal, but when the Landlord removed the dishes the Duke sat back on his chair, and stretched out his legs in front of him.

'I think my bed upstairs will certainly be preferrable to the hard ground under the trees which you suggested earlier today,' he teased.

'We have been very lucky that Mr Travers could bring us here, and I think it was clever of him to say we were a runaway couple,' Valora answered.

'I thought perhaps you would repudiate such an idea, as you disapprove of marriage,' the

Duke said mockingly.

'I did not say I disapparove of it,' Valora corrected. 'I only said it was not something I wanted for myself.'

'Which is, of course, a ridiculous contention. You only make it because you are too young to know your own mind.'

If he intended to provoke her he could not have done so more skilfully.

Valora's eyes flashed at him as she exclaimed:

'I do know my own mind! And I know I have no wish to be a slave to any man!'

'Is that what you think it would be?'

'Of course it would. Women are treated like chattels, and when a man finds his wife boring he can leave her in the country while he goes to London to enjoy himself. No one considers it reprehensible.'

The Duke knew she would be thinking of her mother, and he replied:

'I think a lot of women are not subservient and by perhaps devious means get the upper hand.'

'Only if they use their feminine wiles and allurements in what is an underhand and unsporting manner.'

The Duke raised his eyebrows but his eyes were twinkling as he asked:

'What is unsporting in being alluring to a man?'

'It is wrong to make him do things he would not do otherwise, simply because a woman tempts him,' Valora snapped.

The Duke put back his head and laughed.

'But that is exactly what women have done since the begining of time! What about Eve? What about all those alluring women, whom I am sure you have read about in history? They all got their own way because they were beautiful, and men admired their faces not their brains.'

'You are trying to tell me I should not be intelligent,' Valora replied. 'Quite simply if I was ugly I would not be in the position I am in now.'

Because of what she said it made her think of Sir Mortimer, and the Duke noticed she gave a little shiver.

'Having eluded him,' he said, 'you now have to use the brains on which you set so much store to be free of him for ever.'

'It is not going to be easy,' Valora replied, 'and though I hate to admit it I could not have escaped without the help of a man.'

'Sometimes we have our uses.'

'But of course you have,' Valora said. 'All

I am saying is that I do not want to marry you.'

The Duke thought a little wryly this was not only plain speaking but something he had never heard from a woman before.

He could not remember a time since he had been at Eton when there had not been some woman one way or another scheming to be his wife, or if such a distinction was not for herself, it was for her daughter.

As he thought about it, a whole stream of faces seemed to pass in front of his eyes.

Fair women, dark women, red-heads, and they all appeared in retrospect to have attractive features, and yet the similarity amongst them was unmistakable.

It was there to be read in their eyes—blue, brown, grey, green and hazel—the expression was always the same.

'Greed,' the Duke thought bitterly.

Greed—primarily because he was a Duke, although also he conceded a large number of women desired him as a lover. They were usually those who were not in the position to become the Duchess of Brockenhurst.

At the same time, he had the uncomfortable feeling that they would not have been so keen to risk their reputations with him if he had not been so rich, so important, and the mere fact he was enamoured with them was a feather in their social cap.

The expression on his face must have been somewhat revealing, as Valora said quickly:

'I am sorry...was it...rude of me to say...that?'

'It was at least honest,' the Duke replied.

'That is something I always want to be,' Valora said, 'but at the same time because you have been so kind to me, I do not wish you to think I do not appreciate you as a man.'

'What do you mean by that?' the Duke asked.

She put her head a little on one side as if she was analysing him.

'You are handsome,' she said, 'which I am sure you know without my saying so. You look very strong and you are obviously used to acting quickly.'

'I am prepared to agree to all that,' the Duke replied.

'But I think also,' Valora went on, 'that you have hidden within you things which you would rather not face or remember.'

'What do you mean by that?'

'It is difficult to put into words,' she answered, 'yet I have the feeling you live on the top of life, superficially is probably the right word, while underneath there are many possibilities that are part of you, and yet you pretend they are not there.'

The Duke did not speak for a moment, then he said:

'You are still not making it very clear.'

Valora gave a little sigh.

'I like to think I am good at reading character, but you are rather complex. What I think I am trying to say is that at one time you had beliefs, ambitions and perhaps ideals, but as the years passed you have put them aside, forgotten them, or deliberately suppressed them.'

The Duke was astonished. He knew exactly what Valora was trying to say, though he tried to deny it to himself.

When he had been at Oxford, and then in the War, he and his special friends, especially Freddie, had been filled with idealistic ambitions of how they would change the world.

They had thought that the War would sweep away a lot of the injustices and prejudices that had seemed wrong and restrictive to people who believed in freedom.

England had been fighting for that against the French, and he and his friends had told themselves that when peace came England would move into a new era of prosperity for everyone, not only for the highest in the land, but also for the lowest.

Yet now he knew that after leaving the Army apart from a few speeches in the House of Lords, he had been caught up almost without realising it, in the social whirlpool which was concerned primarily with amusement and the sporting one which aimed only at beating other competitors to the winning-post.

Because he was perturbed, not only by what Valora had said to him, but also by his own thoughts, he pushed his chair back from the table.

'I am sure I can find a great many arguments to refute your analysis of me, but let us keep them for tomorrow. As we have to leave at dawn, the sooner we are in bed the better.'

As if she felt she had upset him, Valora arose quietly to her feet.

'You are right,' she said, 'and thank you very much for all you have done for me. I do not know how I can...ever repay you...which is something I very much...want to do.'

'Suppose we talk about it when we reach York,' the Duke suggested.

He smiled as he spoke and he saw the look of worry that had been in Valora's eyes in case she had annoyed him, vanish. He was also aware of her dimples as she smiled in response.

'Goodnight, Mr Stanton,' she said. 'I shall

say a prayer for you tonight.'

'I am sure it will be very efficacious,' the Duke replied, 'and may I point out that as my fiancee you would address me by my Christian name.'

He lowered his voice as he spoke, and as if she fancied they might be overheard Valora glanced towards the door.

'I am sorry, I will not be careless again,' she said in a voice that only he could hear.

Then she curtsied and went from the room. He heard her footsteps going upstairs.

The Duke went to the stables to see if Samson and Mercury were all right. It was something he had never thought of doing before, as his horses had always been looked after by highly paid and experienced grooms.

Now he found Samson had kicked over the bucket of water beside his manger, and as there was no one about, he had to refill it himself.

There was hay for the horses to eat, but he thought that tomorrow he must buy them some oats to sustain them on what was going to be a long and exhausting ride.

The same applied to Valora, and as he was walking back to the Inn he thought of how well she had behaved all day, and how she had never mentioned that she was stiff or even tired.

"She must however, have been both," the Duke reasoned.

He wondered how she could manage to look so small and frail, and yet apparently have the stamina of an Amazon.

'If she finds my character is difficult to read, I certainly think hers is extremely complex,' he thought as he went up the stairs.

He undressed and got into bed. The goose feathers were soft, and he admitted to himself though he had often slept in much worse conditions during the War, it had been as Freddie had pointed out, ten years ago, now he was older and more fastidious.

Then he was planning how he could get Valora to safety in York, at the same time being half afraid he might fail.

★ ★ ★ ★

The Duke allowed Valora and himself an extra hour in bed, and it was nearly five o'clock when he willed himself to wake, hearing the cocks crowing as he did so.

Once again he got out of bed and dressed himself with some degree of decency before he knocked on her door.

She did not answer, and he walked in to find,

as he had done the previous morning, that she was asleep. This time he went to the bed and spoke:

'Valora!' he said.

She stirred and gave a little cry, then sat up.

'What is the matter...what is wrong?'

'Nothing,' the Duke replied.

He was aware in the light coming through the uncurtained window how lovely she looked.

Her expensive nightgown was very diaphanous and very revealing, and with her hair falling over her shoulders, her eyes a little hazy with sleep, she looked like the princess in a fairy tale.

'I was dreaming that we were...running away...and when you...woke me I thought I was..caught.'

The fear was back in her eyes and the Duke said:

'My Nurse always used to tell me that dreams go by the contrary. I feel sure this one is no exception to the rule.'

Valora gave a deep sigh.

'I hope you are right...is it time to...get up?'

'It is five o'clock.'

'Then we should have left already.'

'I am putting my trust in Bill,' the Duke replied. 'As I am certain he may appear at any moment, I suggest you get dressed.'

He went from the room as he spoke.

As he was finishing his own dressing he was thinking of the whiteness of Valora's skin, and the contrast of the gold in her hair. He was also aware that her figure, which seemed so slim in the dress she had worn last night, had been softly curved beneath the revealing nightgown.

Then he thought to himself that if Valora was not interested in men, he was certainly at this moment not interested in women.

He had almost forgotten that while she was escaping from Sir Mortimer he was escaping from Imogen, or rather Lord Wentover, who he was quite certain would be frantically trying to discover where he had gone.

Thinking of His Lordship made the Duke aware that he could be added to Valora's category of the men she had found so unpleasant.

Not that Wentover, even with his penchant for pretty Cyprians on whom he spent money he did not possess could be compared with the bestiality of Sir Mortimer.

But the Duke suspected that Valora's Father had also disillusioned her considerably in his treatment of her Mother even before he was fool enough to run away with an actor's wife, who was, as the servants would say, "no better than she ought to be."

"Valora has certainly got herself into a nice mess," the Duke thought.

Yet with her strength and his determination he would get her to York, to her Grandfather, whatever obstacles might be put in their way.

He went downstairs to find Valora was there before him, already eating eggs and bacon.

The Duke accepted a large plate of the same food and coffee, which was, if not of the first quality, certainly quite pleasant.

'I hopes everythin' be to yer liking, Sir?' the Proprietor's wife said, as she placed a honeycomb on the table. 'Bill says we were to look after ye, and as us thinks the world o'him we'd do anything for his friends.'

'I am glad to hear you say that,' Valora said. 'I think he is a wonderful man.'

'So do we, Miss,' the Proprietor's wife answered. 'Last winter when things were so bad us thinks as how we couldn't carry on. 'Twas Bill that helped us when there were no one else.'

'Just the sort of thing he would do,' Valora answered.

'I says a prayer every night that God'll bless him for what he does for others,' the Proprietor's wife went on. 'He never discusses it heself, but I've heard tales o' people he's helped all o'er the County, and there be many in need o' help I can tell ye.'

'I am sure there is,' Valora replied. 'You must take care of Bill as you have taken care of us.'

'It's been a pleasure, Miss,' the Proprietor's wife said, 'and I wishes ye both every happiness.'

She smiled at Valora and the Duke before she left the room.

'I told you Bill was a wonderful man,' Valora said. 'It is a waste of his ability to be chased by the Military and have a price on his head when he should be teaching people.'

'Like you?' the Duke asked.

'I am well aware I have a great deal more to learn.'

'When you have learnt it all, what then?'

Valora made a little gesture with the cup she held in her hand.

'One can never learn it all in one lifetime. I think knowledge is like looking up at the sky and trying to count the stars. There are too many, but every one of them is beautiful.'

The Duke was about to reply, when the door opened and the Highwayman came into the room. Valora gave a little cry of delight.

'We were wondering what had happened to you.'

'Sit down and tell us about it,' the Duke suggested.

He pulled out a chair and as he did so, the Innkeeper's wife came into the room with another large plate of bacon and eggs. She put it down in front of him, and set a pot of fresh coffee down on the table.

'Now eat up,' she said in a tone of a mother to a small boy. 'Me husband's giving Bessie some of yer special oats, so don't worry yer head about her.'

'I won't!' the Highwayman replied.

'I thought last night that was something I should have bought for our horses,' the Duke said.

'You can have some of mine,' the Highwayman replied.

'You have done enough for us already,' the Duke answered, 'and I will remember the oats tonight.'

'Tell us what you found out,' Valora interposed, as if she could not wait any longer.

The Highwayman ate a large mouthful of the eggs before he replied.

'No one arrived at the Hall last night, but Walter slept at Slodgbury which is about three miles south.'

He paused to take another mouthful before he went on:

'I thought he would go there. It is the only decent Inn in the neighbourhood, and Mr Walter likes his comfort.'

The Highwayman spoke scathingly.

'He is not far away,' Valora said in an agitated tone. 'We must leave at once.'

'I have an idea,' the Highwayman remarked, 'that he is thinking you would keep to the main road, and may be behind you.'

'Who is with him?' the Duke asked.

'Two men—Giles I imagine, and one of the outriders.'

'They have all been trained to shoot well,' Valora said.

She glanced at the Duke as she spoke, and he knew she was thinking they might easily kill or maim him.

'If you have finished,' he said, 'I think we should be on our way.'

'Wait a minute,' the Highwayman said. 'I have worked out where it would be best for you to stay tonight.'

'You are coming with us?' Valora asked.

He shook his head.

'No, I am going to keep an eye on Walter.'

Valora gave a little cry.

'Be careful, he knows who you are, and would not hesitate to denounce you.'

'I am well aware of that,' the Highwayman said, 'But I owe him something I hope one day to repay.'

'What is that?' Valora asked curiously.

'I suspect—in fact, I am certain, that it was Walter who informed Lord Mount that I was teaching the children on his Estate, and that I had also been asked to give the grown-ups lessons.'

'How do you know it was Walter?' Valora enquired.

'I think it was one of the men from our Estate who went to work on yours, Miss Valora, who informed on me. It was a chap I never trusted, and I am sure that it was he who started the trouble that ruined my life.'

Valora reached out her hand impulsively and put it over his.

'One day perhaps we will be able to make it up to you.'

'I would just like to get even with Walter,' the Highwayman replied.

The Duke had been standing while Valora was talking to the Highwayman, and now she sensed his impatience and jumped to her feet.

'I will not be two minutes while I collect my things,' she said.

When she had left the room the Duke said:

'It is difficult to express my gratitude at all adequately, but I would like you to accept this.'

He put some notes, as he spoke, down on the table beside the Highwayman's breakfast plate. Then as he stiffened and the Duke knew he was going to refuse to take it, he said:

'It is not for you it is for your horse, which I imagine has been working overtime. And if there is anything over for the people you help when they are in need.'

The Highwayman, who had just been about to thrust the money back towards the Duke, hesitated:

'Who has been talking?'

'Just someone who is grateful to you—as we are.'

The Highwayman picked up the notes.

'Very well,' he said. 'I will take them because I may have to pay informers to bring me news of Walter, and all that matters at the moment is that you should get Miss Valora to her Grandfather.'

'That is what I intend to do.'

The note of determination in the Duke's voice was unmistakable.

The Highwayman looked at him speculatively.

'You may think it an impertinence, but I am just wondering how you got mixed up in this mess. Make no mistake, it may be a bloody one before we are finished.'

'It is something I am quite prepared to tell you, and in detail, when we are victorious,' the Duke replied with a smile.

The Highwayman laughed.

'I like you,' he said, 'and though at first I was a bit suspicious as to why you were with Miss Valora, I trust you. Yet seeing how lovely she is, I am not quite certain why.'

The Duke was aware it was one of the most genuine compliments he had ever received.

'Thank you,' he replied, and left the room to pay the Landlord for their lodgings.

CHAPTER 4

After a night which was very like the one they had spent at *'The Magpie'*, they started off early in the morning, with the horses frisky from the oats they had eaten the night before.

The Duke, however, was aware that Valora was looking tired, and he was determined to make it as easy a day for her as possible.

They had both been somewhat exhausted the previous evening when they reached the small village where the Highwayman had directed them to an Inn where they would be safe.

When they sat down to a somewhat indifferent meal, the Duke was aware that Valora was nodding over her food. There was, therefore, none of the intelligent conversation that she had looked forward to, and he had found himself enjoying.

Instead as soon as the meal was over she stumbled upstairs, and by the time the Duke had seen to the horses he was sure she was deep in her dreams.

Now, despite a little shadow under her eyes,

she looked like Spring itself, and her voice had a lilt in it which he had begun to listen for.

The Duke had half hoped the Highwayman would turn up to tell them what was happening at Heverington and if Walter was on their tracks.

But there was no sign of him, and he merely told the Innkeeper the same tale he had used the night before, and swore him to secrecy in case anyone should enquire if they had stayed at his Inn.

The Innkeeper did not seem very interested, and the Duke thought perhaps he thought the story was just to cover up a very different sort of liaison.

His wife however, was more obliging, and when the Duke suggested that they should take something with them that they could eat for their luncheon, she packed them sandwiches of tongue, pressed between bread warm from the oven, and added a small bag of raspberries, which had just begun to turn red in the garden.

'Why did you ask for sandwiches?' Valora asked as they rode off. 'I thought you enjoyed your mug of cider, even though it is not the expensive claret I suspect you are used to.'

'Today we shall be near a town,' the Duke replied, 'and I thought it wise to keep well out of sight.'

'Of course!' Valora exclaimed.

She gave a little sigh.

'Every day I realise I could never have managed this journey without you. How could I have been so lucky as to find you just when I was desperate?'

'Perhaps it was Fate.'

'Do you really think our lives are mapped out for us, and have no choice in the matter?'

The Duke thought for a moment before he replied:

'I believe Fate is what most people call "good luck", and often one needs courage to gamble on it being the right thing, just as I thought it right to knock on your door when I heard you crying, and right for you to trust me to help you escape.'

Valora gave him a smile that was as dazzling as the sunshine.

'That is just the sort of reasonable argument I like to hear,' she replied, 'and it exonerates me from thinking that I am imposing on you, and that you would much rather be riding alone on your journey without the encumbrance of a strange woman.'

'Now you are definitely fishing for compliments,' the Duke answered. 'May I point out that it is a very feminine characterisitic?'

She made a little grimace at him, and then they were riding too swiftly to be able to talk.

It was not quite noon when the Duke pulled Samson to a standstill in a beechwood.

He had glimpsed the spires and towers of the market town he wished to avoid on the horizon, and he thought the sooner they were past it the better. It would take time so it would be best to eat now.

'I am certainly willing to do that,' Valora said, when he explained his reasons for stopping.

He helped her out of the saddle, and then knotted the reins of both horses on their necks, so they could graze any grass there was under the trees.

Then he brought the parcel of sandwiches from his saddle-bag and opened it out, to see that the Innkeeper's wife had included some slices of cheese, wrapped in lettuce leaves.

'It is really quite a feast,' Valora said, 'but the raspberries are rather crushed.'

'I daresay they will taste all right,' the Duke replied.

He leant back against the trunk of a beech tree, and took off his hat.

At the same time, because the Highwayman's abrupt appearance had taught him to be always on the alert, he pulled his pistol from his pocket and laid it on his knee.

'Do not think of Highwaymen lurking in this lovely wood,' Valora admonished him. 'I want to believe it is full of fairies, gnomes and elves digging over the roots of the trees.'

The Duke smiled, and he thought, though he did not say so, she looked like one of the fairy people herself.

She had pulled off her hat, so that the sun coming through the leaves of the beech trees turned her hair to gold, and her eyes seemed to have captured the rays of the sun.

She was looking at the Duke, and after a moment he said:

'What are you thinking about?'

'I was thinking how shocked Mama's friends would be if they knew I was travelling alone with you, and we were not chaperoned at night.'

'Does it worry you?'

'No, of course not. You are not the sort of man I would be frightened of.'

'I have a feeling that is something of an insult,' he Duke said.

Valora laughed.

'Now you are being ridiculous. You do not have that swimmy look in your eyes, and you do not try to touch me with hot flabby hands, as that horrible Sir Mortimer did, and the other men whom Stepmama invited to our house in London.'

'What did you do to avoid them?' the Duke asked.

'I kept out of their way as much as possible,' Valora answered. 'When one man tried to kiss me, I stamped very hard on his foot. He swore, but he never tried it again.'

'I see you are very proficient in taking care of yourself,' the Duke said mockingly.

'I wish that were true! You may think it a strange thing to say, but I think it was because I would have nothing to do with Sir Mortimer that he decided to marry me.'

The Duke knew this was more than likely, and it was clever of Valora to realise it. Then because he knew the idea of Sir Mortimer frightened her, he said lightly:

'We were talking about me, and as that is a subject I am interested in, I suggest we return to it.'

'Unlike most men I have met, you never seem to want to talk about yourself,' Valora replied. 'You know everything about me, but I know nothing about you—except that you are very kind.'

The Duke did not reply and after a moment she asked:

'What do you do when you are not riding to York?'

'As I believe you rather fancy yourself as being perceptive, I suggest you guess,' the Duke replied.

Valora looked at him in the way she had looked at him before when she was analysing his character.

'You are rather puzzling,' she said after a moment.

'Why?'

'Because of the way you walk and give orders I should have thought you were someone of importance, and of course that means rich, but...'

She looked at his boots and the Duke laughed.

'I am well aware,' he said, 'I look a vagabond.

He had thought as he dressed that morning that Jenkins would have been horrified at the state of his clothes.

His riding-jacket, which came from the most expensive tailors in Savile Row, patronised by all the Bucks and Dandies, was badly in need of a brush and a press. His boots were dusty and had lost their polish, and he had that morning put on the last of his clean cravats.

Aloud he said:

'I had a feeling you are somewhat ashamed of me, so I hope tonight we can find an Inn where there is a servant who can improve my appearance—if only by washing my cravats.'

'I will do that,' Valora answered.

'Do you know how?'

'Of course I do. Stepmama demanded the attention not only of her own lady's maid but of all the housemaids and after Papa died and there was no money, I had to look after myself.'

She glanced at the Duke as if to see if he was impressed, and went on:

'Actually I can sew very well, I can wash and press, and I am sure I can polish your boots to make them shine as Papa's used to do.'

'That is certainly something I would never allow you to do,' the Duke replied sharply. 'At the same time, you will undoubtedly make an excellent wife for some fortunate man who cannot afford the luxury of a great number of servants.'

'And he is certainly not going to have me as one,' Valora answered quickly. 'As I have already told you I do not intend to be either a slave or a servant.'

'Then we shall obviously have to try to find you a man who is very wealthy,' the Duke answered.

'You are talking about my marriage to annoy me, and to punish you,' Valora threatened, 'I shall probably not wash your cravats.'

She popped another raspberry in her mouth, and rose saying:

'I must stretch my legs before we start riding again, and perhaps—who knows?—I shall see the fairies dancing over the moss. I assure you I would be far more thrilled by them than I would be by a mere man.'

She walked away and the Duke laughed.

He enjoyed their spirited skirmishes when he teased her, and she always had a ready retort.

At the same time he thought that Freddie would think it extremely "good for his soul" that she obviously did not consider him in the least attractive, nor was he capable of making her heart beat faster.

'Perhaps I am getting old,' he thought, and decided that it was a lowering thought, which had certainly never occurred to him before.

He knew Valora was right in thinking that if anyone knew that she was staying alone at night with a strange man in a country Inn, they would be extremely shocked.

What was more, her reputation would be ruined, and all respectable women would ostracise her as a social pariah.

The Duke was aware this was just as great a danger to her future as was Sir Mortimer, which was another reason why it was absolutely essential that their journey should be kept secret.

He was wondering if when she reached her Grandfather's house he should just leave her at the gate and disappear, when he heard her scream.

It was a scream of horror, and the Duke jumped to his feet clutching his pistol, with his finger on the trigger as he ran in the direction he had seen Valora go.

She was out of sight among the green undergrowth, but as he pushed his way through it he saw the top of her head and a moment later realised, with a sense of relief, she was alone.

It flashed through his mind that she was menaced by a snake, or perhaps a wild animal. Then when he reached her he saw what had made her scream.

She was standing very still, her eyes wide with horror, as she looked to where the Duke saw in a small clearing lay the body of a man!

He could see at first glance why Valora had screamed.

The man was sprawled on the grass and there

was a crimson stain of blood over his white shirt and his coat.

The Duke also saw that he held a pistol in his hand, and that as the blood on his clothing was dry he had obviously been dead for some hours.

The Duke walked past Valora and looking down at the man, saw he was young, looked well bred, and his clothes were expensive.

On his chest, as if he had placed it there carefully before he shot himself, was a piece of paper which read:

'This, Charlotte, is what you have done to me.'

There were some letters and papers scattered on the ground beside him as if he had either been reading them or had thrown them down just before he took his life.

As the Duke stood looking at him, he felt Valora's hand creep into his, and she said in a trembling little voice:

'Is...he...dead?'

'There is nothing whatever we can do for him,' the Duke said firmly, 'so I suggest we go away and forget that we have seen him. We certainly do not wish to be embroiled in any more trouble.'

Valora did not answer, and he saw she was reading the note on the young man's chest.

The Duke turned to leave pulling her by the hand.

'No, wait!' she exclaimed.

'There is nothing we can do,' he answered. 'He shot himself throught the heart and has been dead for some time.'

'How could he do...anything so...foolish?' Valora asked. 'Think what Charlotte...whoever she may be, will...feel.'

'Perhaps she drove him to it,' the Duke replied.

He was still trying to pull Valora away, but she resisted him.

'He is entitled to take his own life, but not to ruin hers.'

'What do you mean?'

'Can you not understand what they will say about her when he is found.'

Valora looked again at the note before she went on:

'He has done that deliberately to hurt her, and all her life people will point a finger at her and say "She killed him". It is cruel...a cruel...unkind thing to do.'

'It is not our business,' the Duke said. 'Come along, Valora, and stop imagining things you know nothing about.'

'I do know that she will have to go on living

with a stigma no one will ever let her forget,' Valora answered.

The Duke did not reply, and she said:

'I realise a little of what it is like to be...ignored and snubbed...because people disapproved of Stepmama. So I understand what will happen to this girl. Her life will be a...hell, perhaps through no...fault of her...own.'

The Duke capitulated.

'Very well,' he said. 'It may be unethical, but if it makes you happy.'

He released Valora's hand and bent down to take the piece of paper from the dead man's chest, and picked up the letters that were scattered on the ground beside him.

He then walked back to Valora, and as he reached her she put out her hand, and once again slipped it into his.

'Thank you...I feel that was a...kind thing to do.'

'The sooner we can get away from here the better,' the Duke said. 'I have no wish to be questioned as to whether I was responsible for that young man's death, as now we have removed the evidence that he killed himself.'

As he spoke the Duke looked down at the letters, and saw they were addressed to The Honourable George Hughes.

He vaguely wondered who owned the family name of Hughes, and then realised that among the letters was a piece of paper that was a marriage licence.

He opened it and found that Honourable George Hughes was the son of Lord Bentford, and he was licensed to marry Charlotte Mayhem, a spinster of the Parish of Wentbury.

He supposed that Charlotte Mayhem had refused, perhaps at the last moment, to marry young Hughes without paternal permission, and in consequence he had shot himself.

Alternatively she might have found someone better, and perhaps explained why she was no longer interested in one of the letters he held in his hand.

Because the Duke thought it a mistake for Valora to dwell on what had happened, he thrust the letters into the pocket of his riding coat and determined that the episode should be forgotten as soon as possible.

'She has enough troubles,' he told himself, 'without adding to them anyone else's.'

At the same time the Duke was aware from Valora's pale face and the stricken look in her eyes that she was upset and shocked by what she had seen.

He imagined, but did not like to ask her, that

she had not seen many people dead, perhaps only her Mother and Father.

But a corpse laid out with hands crossed on the breast, surrounded with flowers and candles, was very different to the young man dead under the trees with blood staining his clothes.

It made the Duke remember that the Highwayman had said the journey might be a bloody one before they had finished.

"The whole thing is turning into a nightmare,' he thought, and forced himself to concentrate on avoiding the town while still moving North,

Soon they were again in the open countryside and the Duke was considering where they should stop for the night when Valora asked:

'What will you do with the letters that you took from that...young man?'

'Burn them.'

'Will you read them first?'

'Certainly not—it would be a most dishonourable thing to do!'

'I expected you would think that, and now we shall never know what happened, and why Charlotte made him do anything so wrong and cowardly.'

'Cowardly?' the Duke questioned.

'Of course it was cowardly to kill himself rather than face living. Life is a gift from God, and however difficult it may be we have no right to...destroy ourselves.'

The Duke glanced at her but did not say anything. Then in a moment she said in a small voice:

'I did...think if I had...married Sir Mortimer I would rather...die.'

'Now you admit it would be a cowardly thing to do, we can concern ourselves with keeping alive, and that means getting to York as quickly as possible,' the Duke said sharply.

They did not talk any more and the Duke found a small village Inn some way from the main road which he thought looked clean and very like the other places in which they had stayed.

It was however somewhat deceptive in that it proved to be larger than it had appeared from the front of the building, and there were other guests staying there.

The Duke, with an air of authority which belied his appearance, managed to procure two of the best rooms with a private parlour.

He thought that the Proprietor looked at him somewhat questioningly, but when he saw Valora his suspicions, if that was what they were, changed and he showed them to their bedrooms with a flourish.

'I am sure this is too grand,' Valora said when she was sure that what she said to the Duke would not be overheard.

'I thought it would be a mistake to withdraw after we had asked for accommodation,' the Duke replied. 'I cannot believe that so far from home there is anyone who will recognise you or me for that matter.'

'I suppose not,' Valora answered a little doubtfully.

The Duke did not explain that his friends would certainly not patronise so insignifcant an Inn, and if they were forced to stay on their way North, would choose one of the larger posting-houses on the main road.

He thought however, just in case there was someone who had seen him on a racecourse or at one of the pugilist mills that he and Freddie attended so often, he would take every precaution.

He therefore made certain there was no one in the passages as he left his bedroom for the private parlour, and decided not to visit the stables again until the other guests were retired to bed.

He did however, discover there was a Valet

of some sort to wait on the guests.

For the first time since they had started on their journey he changed from his riding-breeches into the tight-fitting pantaloons which Jenkins had packed for him.

He had the slippers which had been in his saddle-bag to wear instead of his boots, which he told the servant to clean as best he could.

He also insisted that the man should brush and sponge his coat before, having nothing else to wear, he put it on again.

While he was waiting for it to be returned Valora knocked on his door. He opened it, and she said:

'Give me your cravats, I will wash them now and then they will be dry by the morning. You must be careful not to wear them if they are damp or they will give you a stiff neck.'

'You are very solicitous about my health,' the Duke said mockingly.

'I am saving myself from having to nurse you,' she flashed.

He laughed, but handed her the cravats, thinking what was so obviously a woman's work was as good for her soul as his in fending for himself.

"God knows why I ever got into this position,' he thought, and was suddenly aware that he was enjoying himself.

Not once since leaving London except the first afternoon when he had ridden alone, had he been bored.

For a moment he queried whether that was the truth, and then he knew he could say honestly with his hand on his heart that he felt more alive than he had done for years.

'It is the element of danger in the whole thing,' he decided but he knew it was because he enjoyed being with Valora.

She was certainly different from any woman he had ever known before, and though he knew very little about, and practically no acquaintance with young girls, he was quite certain she was unique.

There was no comparison between her and the rather vacant debutantes who stood beside their mothers in ballrooms waiting to be invited to a dance by some goofish young man.

When he had thought about it the Duke knew that what was extraordinary was that Valora did not seem embarrassed by the fact she was alone with him, not was she coy or in any way self-conscious.

In some ways, when they were arguing with each other, he thought he might have been talking to Freddie.

He almost forgot she was a woman—and a very young one at that—as he endeavoured to prove his point or refute some statement she had made.

Then he remembered how she had looked that second morning when he had called her and she had sat up in bed, and how the outline of her breasts beneath her diaphanous nightgown had made her appear very much a woman.

"One day she will fall in love," the Duke told himself, "and then all this nonsense about never being married will be forgotten."

Because the idea of love was in his mind, he must have conveyed it to hers. For when they had finished dinner in the private parlour Valora said:

'I have been...thinking about the...young man who...killed himself!'

'I told you not to do so,' said the Duke.

'I know you did, but I was wondering why... love, which is surely a gentle and romantic emotion...should make a man so...desperate that he would...kill himself.'

'Love is not always gentle and romantic,' the Duke replied.

Valora looked at him enquiringly as he went on:

'It can be fiery, tempestuous and above all things uncontrollable.'

'Is that...what it...makes you feel?'

'I was talking impersonally—academically if you like.'

'Explain it to me.'

'You can read about it,' the Duke answered. 'Romeo and Juliet died for love; Othello murdered for it; I cannot believe you do not know your Shakespeare.'

'Of course I have read his plays,' Valora answered, 'and I have read Sir Walter Scott's novels, but nothing they wrote about love seemed real...until today. Now I will have to begin to think about it...all over...again.'

'Why? It is something you are determined never to feel.'

'That is what I was...going to ask...you.'

She saw he looked puzzled, and explained:

'When anyone falls in love...does it just happen...and is there...nothing you can do to...prevent it?'

'I suppose so,' the Duke replied.

'Why do you speak like that? Surely you must have been in love?'

'I have thought I was,' the Duke said honestly. 'I have certainly been excited, entranced and fascinated, but I can assure you it has never been so uncontrollable that I have wished to shoot myself.'

'I expect what you are saying,' Valora answered, 'is that you have never been what country people call "crossed by love.".'

The Duke laughed.

'Perhaps that is true.'

'No lovely lady has...killed herself for...you?'

'Certainly not.'

'Then what is love? Why does it mean so... much to some people and not so much to... others?'

There was a faraway expression in her eyes which the Duke found rather touching. In a serious tone, which he had not used before, he said:

'I think everyone wants an ideal love, which is hard to find. It is an ideal we all seek, even though we are unaware of it. After all, it is natural for a man to try and find what the Greeks thought of as "the other part of himself".'

'Of course, now I understand!' Valora cried. 'I remember the legend that the gods cut the first human being they made in half, and called them man and woman, and ever since they have tried to find each other and be complete again.'

'That answers your question,' the Duke said.

'But...suppose one never...finds one's...other half?'

'Then you have to make do with the second best.'

'No...no!' Valora cried. 'That would be wrong...and spoil everything.'

The Duke sat back in his chair to look at her.

'Now I have given you a new quest,' he said. 'Instead of seeking knowledge you must seek the man who the gods chose for you a million years ago. Perhaps you have been travelling towards each other, and one day you will meet. Then you will never be lonely or afraid again.'

As he spoke the Duke was astonished at his own words, which had come into his head involuntarily as if from some outside source.

He thought they were a part of the enchantment that had been his ever since he had started on this mad journey—first because he had accepted Freddie's wager and then in saving Valora.

She looked so lovely in her simple white dress, as she sat listening to him with her elbows on the table, with her face cupped in her small hands.

Her attitude was that of a child at her lessons. The Duke was suddenly palpitatingly aware that she was very much a woman.

He had a sudden impulse to touch her bare arms and her neck, to see if her skin was as soft as it looked. Then he shied away from the idea of admitting he wanted to kiss her.

Yet he knew because she was so innocent, so unawakened, that her lips would be very soft and sweet, and he had an almost overwhelming desire to be the first man to kiss her and feel her mouth beneath his.

He could imagine nothing more thrilling than to awaken a response in her.

But he knew it was something he must not do.

It would be, he told himself, extremely wrong, and certainly dishonourable, to approach her when he had promised to protect her and take her safely to York.

What was more, he was quite certain if he revealed such feelings in any way she would run away from him as she had run away from Sir Mortimer.

As he felt emotions which were for a moment uncontrollable rising in him, he got up abruptly from the table to walk to the diamond casement window to look out onto the untidy garden.

'It is getting late, Valora,' he said almost harshly. 'I think it is time you went to bed.'

'But I want to go on talking to you,' she replied. 'I never thought I should find a man who knew so much about the things which interest me, and not be concerned merely with horses and cards.'

'You accuse me of being cynical,' the Duke answered, 'but I think that is what you are being. I am sure most men know a great many other things than the two subjects which you condemn so wholeheartedly.'

'I do not condemn them,' Valora retorted. 'I only say that to talk of nothing else is rather like eating suet pudding day in, day out, when one is longing for something more interesting.'

'Then as I want you to go to bed, I will now talk about horses until they bore you.'

'I would not be bored if you tell me about Samson. He is the most magnificent stallion I have ever seen.'

'I am quite prepared to congratulate you on acquiring an animal as fine as Mercury,' the Duke said, 'and I realise he means a great deal to you.'

'I have had him since a foal and I love him more than anything else in the world,' Valora answered.

The way she spoke and the sudden light in her eyes made the Duke feel again an uncontrollable desire to kiss her. He knew too that he wanted her to say that she loved him more than anything else in the world.

Then he told himself it had been a mistake to drink so much of the claret that had been served at dinner, and even worse to order a brandy to follow it.

'If you are not going to bed, Valora, I am,' he said, as he walked towards the door.

When he reached it he heard voices outside, and for a moment he forgot everything except the fear that they might be discovered.

He had half opened the door as he spoke, and now he closed it, leaving only a crack through which he could see two women and two men leaving the Dining hall and ascending the stairs.

He watched them, and decided they were ordinary middle-class travellers, doubtless journeying from one town to another, perhaps on business or to visit friends.

He watched them until they reached the top of the stairs, and then heard them walk along the passage to the two rooms situated on the same floor as Valora and himself, facing the front of the Inn.

When they were out of sight he turned back to see Valora still sitting at the table, and watching him apprehensively.

'Is it all...right?' she asked in a whisper.

'Quite all right,' the Duke replied. 'But we must not get careless, Valora. I think now it was a mistake to stay here, and we must set off early in the morning.'

She did not reply, but rose from her chair as he went on:

'We have one more night, I reckon, before we reach York, and you will be safe.'

'Then...what will.. you do?'

Valora came nearer to him as she spoke, and now she looked up at him. As her eyes met his, the Duke felt once again an overwhelming desire to take her in his arms.

It was so insistent, so imperative, that he could feel a throbbing in his temples, and a frantic beating of his heart which was more intense, more insistent, than he had ever known in his life before.

Only an iron control, which he had learned in the Army, prevented him from putting his arms around Valora, and pulling her roughly against him.

He wanted her—he wanted her in a way that made him feel that nothing else in the world was of any consequence. The danger they were in, the need to reach York and safety, were all swept away by a flood-tide which he felt must overwhelm him.

As he was aware she was still looking at him enquiringly he said harshly:

'For God's sake go to bed, unless you want to be dragged back to marry Heverington!'

He felt as he spoke as if he had struck something small and defenceless.

He saw the fear come back into her eyes, before she pulled open the door and he heard her footsteps running swiftly up the uncarpeted stairs towards her bedroom.

★ ★ ★ ★

If the Duke slept badly, so did Valora.

All she could think about was the harsh note in his voice and the darkness in his eyes when he had told her to go to bed. She could not understand why he was angry, or what she could have done to upset him.

She had looked forward so much to their dinner alone together, and while she was changing she had told herself there were a hundred questions she wanted to ask.

She had never before known how exciting it was to talk to a man who was near her own age, and who spoke to her as if she was his intellectual equal.

To her father she had always been a child, and to her teacher like Mr Travers she had been very much a pupil whose opinion, unless it was supported by facts, they did not find very interesting.

They wanted to lecture and not to listen.

All the other men she had met, young and old, had only paid her compliments and, as she had told the Duke, had tried to touch her.

She did not know quite why they revolted her, though now she thought of what the Duke had said before he had grown angry; that what she wanted was ideal love.

It had never struck her for some reason she could not quite understand, that marriage could be like that—a love that was beautiful and as mystic as the magic she sensed in the woods and the tales she told herself that were much more vivid than those she could read in books.

She had sought knowledge since her mother told her she needed it. But she thought now that it should be knowledge of people as well as of intellectual subjects.

She suddenly felt her whole attitude to life was ignorant and rather foolish.

She had been so positive that because she loathed Sir Mortimer she would never marry, and submit to being treated as casually as her father had treated her mother when she was ill, when he had gone off adventuring on his own.

Because she was a child and intensely loyal to those she loved, she worried terribly that her mother had been unhappy, even though she pretended to take it with a philosophical spirit.

'Men will be men, Valora,' she would say, 'as you will find out for yourself when you are older.'

'Why does Papa not take you to London with him?' Valora would enquire.

'Because I am not well enough to do all the things he wants to do,' her mother would reply miserably. 'Men want women who are well enough to dance, to ride and...to laugh with... them.'

There had been a pause before her mother had said the last words and Valora felt now with renewed perception that what she had really been going to say was "to ride, to laugh and to love them."

Thinking of her father with his abounding good health and high spirits, she thought perhaps it had been frustrating for him to have a wife who had not given him the son he had wanted so desperately and who was always a semi-invalid.

He obviously wanted her mother to accompany him to the races, to appear at the Hunt Balls, and of course to take part in all the sporting activities which occupied his days.

But looking back, Valora thought that what he had minded more than anything else was when he had to dine alone.

'Damn it all, Elizabeth,' she had heard him say once to her mother, 'surely you can come down and dine with me. If there is one thing that bores me to extinction, it is eating alone.'

'I wish I could, darling,' her mother had replied, 'but I feel so weak, and you know that I am unable to eat things that do not agree with me.'

'Then I will have to find someone else, won't I!' her father had answered in what she had thought was a disagreeable tone.

He slammed the bedroom door before he went downstairs to the Dining-Room, and the next day he left for London.

All through her childhood she resented him, and thought him unkind, but now she thought that perhaps he had been looking for the other half of himself, although certainly there was nothing idealistic about her Stepmother.

Yet in a way Valora supposed she had given her father something he wanted.

She remembered how he looked at her and

how, if she entered a room unexpectedly, she would find him kissing his new wife in a way that made her feel somehow embarrassed.

He had also bought her Stepmother everything she had wanted, although she had never stopped asking for more.

That explained why there had been no money when he died.

"Was Papa really in love with her?" Valora asked herself in the darkness of the Inn bedroom.

Because it seemed important for her to know the answer, she wanted to get out of bed and go into the room next door and ask kind Mr Stanton to explain to her what she was trying to understand.

'He knows so much about everything,' she murmured.

Then she felt herself wince again because of the harsh way he had spoken.

"I suppose I bore him," she thought, "because I am so ignorant and foolish about things like marriage and love.'

It was almost like a physical pain to think she did not please him.

Then it suddenly struck her, because he was so handsome, so strong, and so clever that there must have been many women who found him irresistibly attractive.

She wondered why he was not married, and why he was making this journey alone.

"It is lucky for me," Valora told herself.

Then she was sure he was beginning to find her a bore, and as she had feared in the first place an encumbrance.

'What can I do to please him?' she asked herself.

She remembered they had only one more night together, and she felt as if time was slipping through her fingers and she could not hold on to it.

"Once we have reached York I shall never see him again," Valora told herself.

Quite unexpectedly but of course, because she was so tired, the tears began to run down her face.

CHAPTER 5

The Duke had taken himself to task during the night for being disagreeable.

Then he felt ashamed when the Valet came into the room with his boots somewhat indifferently cleaned, but with three cravats, washed and with no more than the proper amount of starching, exactly as Jenkins might have produced them.

Because he thought it was the least he could do to show his appreciation, the Duke tied his cravat in a more complicated and fashionable style than he had done hitherto on the journey.

Then he went downstairs to breakfast to apologise to Valora, and determined to make her day a happy one.

He also told himself that once he reached York his feelings for her might alter, and she would no longer attract him so violently as she had done last night.

He thought the reason was partly that he had never before been alone with a woman for so long unless he was making love to her.

He was also inclined to attribute the intensity of his feelings to the fact that he was in better health and more full of energy than he had been for a long time.

The Landlord brought him his breakfast almost as soon as he was sitting at the table. To the Duke's surprise Valora did not appear.

He was not worried that she had disappeared or was ill, because he had heard her moving about in her room while he was dressing and talking to someone else, who he imagined was a chambermaid.

He did, however, glance at his watch two or three times before, as he was finishing his coffee, she came into the parlour.

He was just about to ask her what had kept her, when she came to his side as he rose, to say:

'Would you please give me some money!'

The Duke raised his eyebrows, but he did not speak, and she added quickly:

'I do not want to take more than you can... afford to give me, and I am sure Grandpapa will...pay you back when we...reach him.'

'Why do you want money at this moment?' the Duke asked.

He thought Valora would reply that it was for the chambermaid who had been helping her. To his surprise she hesitated and looked down in what he thought was an embarrassed manner.

'I hope we have no secrets from each other, at any rate none that concern our journey,' he said quietly.

'It is for the...maid who helped me with your cravats,' Valora replied. 'She is very...worried about...herself.'

The way Valora spoke made the Duke sure he knew the answer to his question, but he waited, and after a moment she said with the colour rising in her cheeks.

'She is having a...baby and she will not...be employed here any...longer. She does not...know where she will...go.'

'Then I presume she is not married!' the Duke remarked cynically.

Valora lifted her eyes to his.

'How did you guess?'

The Duke desisted from saying it was not only the oldest story in the world, but one which chambermaids beggars and women of all sorts and condition used to extract money from the soft-hearted.

'How much do you want?' he asked.

'I feel it is wrong of me to ask you to pay when it is I who wish to be charitable,' Valora repled. 'But could you possibly...spare two or three guineas?'

The Duke put his hand in his pocket and drew out three golden guineas, which he held out in the palm of his hand.

Valora took them from him saying:

'Thank you, it is very kind, and I promise the money will be returned to you.'

She reached the door when the Duke said:

'I think we should hurry. We are leaving it later than we usually do.'

'I will only be a minute or so,' Valora replied.

He heard her running up the stairs and she joined him a few minutes later, and without speaking sat down at the breakfast-table and began to eat quickly.

'I will see to the horses,' the Duke said, and went out to the Stables.

Despite the fact that Valora had left her coffee because it was too hot to drink, by the time they left the Inn the servants were already cleaning the doorstep, the Ostlers were rubbing down the horses, and the Duke hoped apprehensively that none of the guests would be awake to see them go.

He however said nothing to Valora, and they rode swiftly across the fields and unenclosed land, all the time heading North.

It was a lovely day with a heat haze over the

lower part of the valley. The sun when it rose promised that later it would be very hot.

The horses were fresh and the Duke pushed Samson a little, feeling it imperative they should make up for lost time, although he told himself it was unnecessary.

At the same time he had learned in the War to trust his sixth sense which in some strange way had always alerted him when there was anything unexpectedly dangerous to be encountered.

He did, however, wonder now if his presentiment was anything more than a new awareness of Valora's attractions, and that he must get her to safety.

He was sure they had already travelled the greater part of the way, but because he was not on the Great North Road where there were milestones, he had no precise idea how far they were from York.

He might, of course, have asked at the Inn, but he told himself there was no point in letting the Landlord know where they were going, just in case by some unfortuante chance Walter, if he was still in pursuit of them, should ask questions at an Inn in which they had stayed.

"It cannot be so very far," he calculated, and

kept the horses galloping at full speed for longer than he usually did.

At noon he decided they should have luncheon, which once again he had taken the precaution to order and carry with them.

This time, because the Inn was of a better quality than those they had stayed in previously, he had asked for a variety of cold meats the night before he went to bed, and also fruit which had been offered them at dinner-time.

He had even found on the wine-list a wine, which if chilled, he thought would be drinkable, and when he saw a small stream winding through some lush meadowland, he decided it would make a natural wine-cooler.

He therefore stopped Samson under a large weeping willow and as he dismounted Valora exclaimed in delight:

'This is a lovely place for us to eat. I was hoping you would want to stop here.'

'At least no one can approach us unawares,' the Duke replied.

As he spoke he looked at the meadowland bright with cuckoo flowers, marigolds and buttercups, stretching for a long distance on each side of the stream.

Valora laughed.

'There might be Red Indians creeping

towards us through the grass.'

'And there might be crocodiles in the stream,' the Duke replied, 'but I rather doubt it.'

As he spoke he took the wine from his saddle-bag and bent over the bank to put it securely in the water.

When he turned round Valora had brought the food from his saddle and opened the packet in which it was contained.

She then took off her hat and the jacket of her habit.

She was wearing a white lawn blouse which the Duke saw revealed the curves of her breast, and he also perceived that on it were fastened three brooches.

There were three little diamond stars varing in size, and he thought they were somehow very appropriate for Valora.

She must have followed the direction of his eyes, and as if he had asked the question, she said:

'They were Mama's, and I had to hide them from my Stepmother, otherwise she would have taken them away from me.'

'That was clever of you,' the Duke smiled.

But as he spoke he was aware from long experience that the diamond stars, while very attractive, especially when a woman wore them in her hair, were not particularly valuable and he hoped that Valora's Grandfather would be rich enough to keep her in comfort.

Another idea presented itself to his mind, but he thrust it away from him, and said aloud:

'As you have made yourself so comfortable and the sun is becoming overwhelmingly hot, will you allow me to remove my riding-coat?'

'Of course,' Valora replied, with a smile.

'I have not thanked you yet for my cravats,' the Duke said. 'I have never had them better washed or starched to exactly the right stiffness as prescribed by Beau Brummel.'

'I am glad you are pleased,' Valora replied. 'Do you aspire to be a Dandy?'

'Certainly not!' the Duke said positively.

'I think you could be one,' Valora went on, 'especially when you tie your cravat as well as you have done this morning.'

'Dandies are affected, frivolous creatures,' the Duke said. 'If you like to call me a Beau or a Corinthian, that is quite different.'

'I am sure you are a Corinthian from the way you ride,' Valora answered. 'But are they not all very important aristocrats?'

The way she asked the question made the Duke aware that it had not occurred to her he was in a position to associate with such lofty social figures.

He told himself that once again he was facing the truth in a blunt fashion.

It was obvious that Valora was not in the least suspicious that he might be other than an ordinary, somewhat impoverished country gentleman.

He was aware how Freddie would laugh if he knew he almost felt piqued that his real identity was not more obvious.

'This again is good for my soul,' he told himself wryly, as he helped himself to the food which was certainly better than anything else they had eaten on previous days.

The wine when it was cooled seemed very enjoyable, but the Duke was not certain whether it was the wine itself, or the sight of Valora seated by the side of the stream, with the full skirt of her habit billowing out around her, and looking like a flower.

She was watching the water moving crystal clear over the stony bottom, the birds flying down to drink from it, and the sunshine glittering golden to make the whole picture seem somehow enchanting.

'That is what I am,' the Duke told himself, 'enchanted.'

Then he thought cynically it was doubtless

an enchantment that would vanish as soon as he got back to civilisation.

Then watching Valora's face he realised she was worried about something.

'What is troubling you?' he asked.

'I was thinking of that poor woman at the Inn.'

'You helped her—I should not add her troubles to your own.'

'She was so grateful for the money...there were tears in her eyes,' Valora said.

She looked down at the stream as if she was shy, before she added:

'But there...is...something I do not...understand.'

'What was that?' the Duke asked.

He was not particularly interested, as he was thinking how beautiful Valora's little straight nose was silhouetted against the trees on the opposite bank.

'I enquired,' Valora said in a very small voice, 'why she did not...ask the...father of her...child to...help her.'

She stopped speaking, then after a palpable pause the Duke asked:

'What did she reply?'

'She...said,' Valora answered, and the words were almost inaudible, 'that she did not...know who he...was.'

There was silence, and then she added:

'I do not...understand how could she not...know, but that is what she...said, and so I would like you to...explain how a...woman begins to...have a...baby.'

She looked up at the Duke as she spoke, and he saw her eyes wide, troubled and very innocent.

For a moment he was astonished she should be so ignorant. Then as he wondered how he could possibly answer her, he knew he was in love!

A strange feeling swept over him and, because it was something he had never felt before for any woman, he recognised it instantly for what it was.

It was love that made him want to protect Valora, not only from the men who were following her, from a husband as bestial as Sir Mortimer, but also from a knowledge of the world that might hurt or shock her.

Never before in his life had the Duke felt the urge to protect a woman, and never before had he known that he not only desired one but felt as if she was something sacred.

It all swept over him like a flash of lightning, or a shaft of sunlight, and he was aware that

Valora's artless question had awakened a chivalry that had lain dormant within him for years.

Because ladies in the social world in which he moved had a freedom of speech and a looseness of morals introduced by the King, which was very different from the behaviour of his mother's generation, the Duke had grown to expect nothing else.

The women he knew were sometimes as outrageous in what they said as they were in their behaviour.

It had never crossed his mind before that any one of them would be ignorant about the love-making between a man and a woman, or that innocence was a desirable quality in itself.

Yet now that he looked into Valora's eyes, and saw how puzzled and bewildered she was, he felt as if she was a saint that he must place on a shrine in his heart, or perhaps a small angel who must not on any count, be contaminated by the world.

'I love her,' he told himself, 'and she is everything I have been looking for in my life. I have been bored and disillusioned because I could not find her.'

She was waiting for his reply and he longed to put his arms around her and tell her he would look after her and keep her safe, not only from physical danger but from everything that worried her in her mind.

But he knew it was too soon!

Men had frightened and shocked her, and though she trusted him the Duke was well aware that she talked to him impersonally.

In fact, her question might have been directed to a father or a brother, but certainly not to a man for whom she had any deep feeling.

'I understand what is troubling you,' he said at length quietly, 'but because I feel we must move on, can we talk about it another time?'

The expression in Valora's eyes altered, and she looked down again at the stream.

'Yes, of course,' she said, 'but it is so lovely here I wish we could stay longer.'

'Perhaps one day we will come back,' the Duke replied, 'or find another enchanted place just like it.'

'Enchanted!' Valora exclaimed. 'That is the right word! That is just what I have been feeling it really is.'

'And so have I,' the Duke replied.

Her eyes lit up as she went on:

'Do you really think that, or are you just saying it to please me?'

'I think you must realise by now,' he

answered, 'that I try to tell the truth. I think it would be an insult to our *friendship* to do anything else.'

He had deliberately accentuated the word "friendship".

Valora responded with a smile as she said:

'But of course friends must always be honest and frank with each other, and we are friends really and truly...are we not?'

She had risen to her feet as she spoke, as the Duke had risen to his, and it was with difficulty he resisted an impulse to put his arms around her and tell her what he felt was not friendship but something very much deeper. Instead he said:

'Really and truly, cross my heart!'

Valora gave a chuckle of delight at his words and put her hat on her head. Then as she picked up her jacket she asked:

'Shall we ride as we are? It is very hot.'

'I think there are few people about who would criticise us for looking unconventional,' the Duke replied.

'No,' she answered, 'and every mile we are getting further and further away from anything that might be horrid and frightening.'

'I am sure we have crossed the border into a new and uncharted land,' the Duke said lightly, and hoped as he spoke it was the truth.

He still however unpredictably, had an unexplained presentiment of danger, and despite the heat they moved quickly with the horses responding to what was asked of them.

They had been riding for some hours when Mercury suddenly slowed down, and Valora gave an exclamation. She was behind the Duke and he looked back.

'What is it?' he asked.

'I think Mercury has picked up a stone in his hoof.'

Valora would have dismounted but the Duke prevented her, saying:

'Hold Samson's bridle and let me see.'

As he jumped to the ground he hoped fervently that Mercury had not gone lame.

Nothing could be more disastrous at this moment, and though he thought it unlikely as they had been moving over meadowland that was not infested with rabbit-holes, there was the possibility of a strained tendon.

Feeling apprehensive, he picked up Mercury's hind hoof, and saw that Valora was right. There was a stone wedged beneath the shoe, and the Duke walked back to his saddle.

When he was riding he carried in his saddle-pocket a special instrument for removing stones from horses' hooves.

So many of the country roads were in bad repair, especially after rainy weather or a winter storm which dispersed the dust, that it was easy for a horse to pick up a stone, which would make him lame until it was extracted.

Knowing what he had to do, Valora slipped from the saddle and stood holding Mercury by the bridle, patting his neck and talking to him in case he was frightened.

Not that what the Duke was about to do would hurt him, it was only that he might be nervous at being handled by a stranger. He could buck or rear, or make things difficult just being restless.

'You are a silly boy to delay us,' she said, talking to him in a soft voice which made Mercury nuzzle his nose against her.

The Duke tried to extract the stone, but found it firmly wedged. He straightened his back, and Valora asked:

'Have you done it?'

'Not yet,' the Duke replied. 'It is rather complicated but I will try again.'

This was another task he had not attempted for a long time, and he wondered if he was being singularly inept, or if the stone was more difficult than might have been expected.

Then as he probed the stone came away, but so did the shoe. He swore softly beneath his breath, and though Valora had not heard what he said, she sensed his annoyance.

'What is the matter?'

'We shall have to find a blacksmith.'

'There is sure to be one not far away,' Valora replied confidently.

'I hope so,' the Duke answered.

Carrying the horseshoe in his hand, he came to Valora's side saying:

'We will take it easy, and Mercury will come to no harm without a shoe on this soft ground, but it is essential he should have one before we go very much further.'

'Mercury is very apologetic for being a nuisance!'

'I am sure he realises that it is through no fault of his own, and perhaps the responsibility lies with the last blacksmith who shod him.'

'I hope not,' Valora answered. 'He is a dear old man who attended to all Papa's horses, and always talked as if he was a Doctor and they were his patients.'

'Then I hope we find one of his kind in the next village,' the Duke replied and they rode on.

Valora was not in the least perturbed that

they could not travel as fast as they had in the morning.

All the time they had been galloping with an urgency which surprised her, she had been thinking time was slipping away and that once they reached York she might never see the Duke again.

She had been certain when she awoke from a fretful sleep that he was longing to be free from the responsibility of taking her to her Grandfather, and to be able to concentrate on his own concerns.

As he had not volunteered any information as to why he was going to York, she felt somehow it would be bad manners to ask him anything that was too personal.

Now when she thought about it, she realised he had never talked about his family, his home, or even his friends.

"I expect he is naturally reserved," she thought to herself, "or else he has no wish to confide in me."

All the same, she wanted to know if he had brothers and sisters, if his mother and father were alive and where they lived.

All she really knew was that, like herself, he had no wish to be married, and that no one could have been kinder or more considerate than he had been when she had been utterly in despair.

'He is very wonderful,' she told herself now as they rode side by side, the Duke holding in Samson to keep pace with Mercury.

In his shirt sleeves without a coat he looked, she thought, stronger and more masculine than he had ever done before.

Under her eyelashes she glanced at his classical profile, as he stared ahead looking for a village where he hoped to find a blacksmith.

Then she noticed the broadness of his shoulders, and thought she could almost see a rippling of his muscles under the thin lawn of his shirt. His waist was small, and he rode a horse as if he was a part of it.

Valora was aware that astride such a magnificent black stallion as Samson, man and beast made a picture that might have stepped straight out of mythology.

"He is god-like," she thought.

Then she remembered that the gods themselves had come down to earth because they wished to behave like men, and enjoy the pleasures with which mankind was blessed, especially that of love.

Valora looked ahead again, away from the Duke.

She was conscious of a very strange feeling within her, a feeling she could not explain to herself. It was different from anything she had known before. It was something like a yearning, and yet more intense.

At the same time she was conscious of her heart beating in her breast and an odd constriction in her throat.

"Perhaps it was the wine I drank at luncheon which makes me feel like this,' Valora told herself, but she knew that was not really the explanation.

'There is a village!' the Duke exclaimed.

Valora saw above the trees a spire of a Church, and a few seconds later, several chimney-pots.

'Wish or rather pray hard,' the Duke said, 'that there will be a blacksmith here with a forge, and that he is at home.'

Valora had lived in the country and knew that blacksmiths were often away visiting farms or a nobleman's Stables and sometimes village horses would have to wait days or even weeks before he could attend to them.

Because the Duke had told her to do so, she did send up a little prayer in her heart that the blacksmith was there. At the same time she knew a delay would not perturb her.

To reach the village they left the meadowland and found themselves on a road that might have been a main one, which obviously passed through the centre of the village itself.

First there were a number of quite attractive cottages, with diamond paned windows and twisted Elizabethan chimneys; then there was a shop, bow-fronted, outside which there stood several women with baskets on their arms.

Beyond, on the opposite side of the road there was a Churchyard with a lych-gate, and quite a number of people passing through it.

The Duke was just about to draw in Samson and ask if there was a blacksmith's shop, when Valora gave a cry and pointed ahead of them.

Almost exactly opposite the Church she could see a horse being held in a large open doorway, and beyond it the flaring light of a forge.

'We are in luck,' the Duke said quietly, and they rode on till they reached the smithy.

The blacksmith was a huge man, past middle-age but still with the muscles of a prize-fighter. He was just finishing shoeing a horse, and a man was holding another one by the bridle.

The blacksmith glanced up at the Duke as he appeared in the entrance, realised he was a gentleman, and said:

'Oi'll not keep ye long, Sir. This customer be ready t'leave.'

He took the horse's hoof off his knee as he spoke, and put it down on the ground. As he rose to a great height, the owner said:

'Thank 'e, Jim!' and slapped a shilling down on the side of the forge.

The Duke went out into the road to where Valora was standing holding both Samson and Mercury.

'Your prayers are very efficacious,' he said. 'We have not only found a blacksmith, but he is free to fix Mecury's shoe. It should not take long.'

Valora smiled at him, as he took Mercury from her and led him into the forge.

Mercury was a little nervous, but the Duke handled him expertly, and as he had often been shoed before, after a moment or so he was still.

Outside, Valora was aware that a service was taking place in the Church, and she thought it must be a wedding.

She could hear the music of an organ and boys' voices singing a hymn that was one commonly sung at weddings.

She was wondering what the bride was like, if she was very happy and if she really wanted to marry the man to whom she was being wed, when suddenly she heard the sound of hooves.

Looking back the way she and the Duke had come she saw a horse travelling at a tremendous speed down the road towards her.

She was watching the man riding it with no great interest, when as he drew near she was aware there was something familiar about him.

She stared, thinking she must be mistaken.

Then as he drew nearer still she saw it was Mr Travers! Instinctively she put up her hand to stop him, stepping further out into the road as she did so, while still holding on to Samson's bridle.

He did not see her at first, then she saw by the expression on his face he was surprised, and he drew in Bessie abruptly, pulling her back on her haunches.

Then as the mare came to a standstill, he flung himself from the saddle saying in a low, insistent voice:

'What are you doing here?—where is Stanton?'

'He is inside,' Valora replied, indicating with her hand the blacksmith's shop.

The Highwayman thrust Bessie's bridle into Valora's hand, and walked quickly into the forge.

The Duke was as surprised to see him as

Valora had been.

'Where have you been?' he began to ask.

Then as he saw the expression on the Highwayman's face he checked the words.

Mr Travers glanced at the blacksmith.

'I must speak to you!' he said in a low voice.

The Duke knew it would be a mistake to talk in front of a stranger.

'Get Valora to hold Mercury,' he said.

The Highwayman understood, and went outside to take Samson and Bessie from Valora.

'Stanton wants you to hold Mercury,' he said without explanation.

Because she knew something serious must have happened, Valora ran into the forge to take Mercury from the Duke.

He walked quickly out to the Highwayman.

'What is wrong?'

'Walter and Giles are just behind me,' the Highwayman replied. 'I anticipated you would be further ahead than this.'

'We have been somewhat dilatory,' the Duke answered.

'Which is unfortunate,' the Highwayman said. 'They found out where you stayed the night before last, and when I learned at *"The Fox and Goose"*, where you rested last night, that you left at five o'clock this morning, I expected you to be a good deal further on than this.'

'Do you think they are coming this way?' the Duke asked.

'You are on the main road,' the Highwayman replied.

The Duke's lips tightened.

'How far are they behind?'

'Perhaps ten minutes.'

'Two of them?'

'The Outrider was ill, so there are only Walter and Giles!'

The Duke glanced back at the forge, and he knew it would be several minutes more before Mercury's shoe was firmly fixed on his hoof. He wondered desperately what he should do.

He thought they might hide somewhere in the village. Then he saw that while they had been in the forge a number of people had begun to congregate outside the lych-gate.

There were three women with their shopping baskets, another woman with several small children, and half a dozen boys who obviously had nothing better to do.

As the Duke looked at them he saw they were all watching the Church door, and at that moment the bride appeared, wearing a traditional white dress, the veil thrown back from her face.

She was a buxom apple-cheeked girl, perhaps the daughter of a local farmer, and her bridegroom was looking hot and flushed which was obviously due to the tightness of his cravat.

They were followed by their parents and several friends all beaming with the benevolent goodwill which a wedding invariably evokes.

As the bridal couple reached the lych-gate, the farmer's gig, drawn by a horse, decorated with a wreath of wild flowers, drew up outside and the bride and groom scrambled into it.

There were cries of "Good Luck!" and "God Bless!" from the women, and somewhat ironical cheers from the small boys, who ran beside the gig as it started off down the road.

The wedding-breakfast was obviously being held not far away, as the parents and friends began to walk quickly in the direction the gig had taken.

'I think you will have to run for it,' the Highwayman said.

There was no doubt from the tone of his voice he was uneasy.

'I have a better idea,' the Duke replied.

Putting the bridle of the two horses into

Highwayman's hand, he walked into the forge.

'There Oi've made a good job o'it,' the blacksmith said in a tone of satisfaction. 'Ye have a fine 'orse here, Sir. 'E won't give ye no trouble for th' next 'undred miles.'

He laughed at his joke, and then looked with delight at the half guinea the Duke had put down on the forge.

'Thank ye,' he said briefly.

The Duke had taken the bridle from Valora and pulled Mercury quickly out of the forge. He took him outside and handed the reins over to the Highwayman.

'Put the horses somewhere where they won't stray,' he ordered. 'I expect there are stables attached to the forge—there usually are. Then follow us into the Church.'

The Highwayman gave him a questioning look. Then he said:

'If it comes to a fight, Walter is mine!'

The Duke did not wait to reply. He merely put his hand under Valora's arm and took her through the lych-gate which was empty of sightseers, and up a short gravel path to the Church door.

'Where are we...going?' she asked in a whisper.

She had guessed without being told what the

Highwayman had related to the Duke, and now the terror that she might be captured and taken back to Heverington and Sir Mortimer had returned.

It swept away everything but a frantic need to hang onto the Duke with both hands and beg him to save her.

They reached the Church door, and as the Duke walked inside still holding her by the arm, she thought perhaps he intended to seek sanctuary in the Church, as criminals had been able to do in the past to escape their pursuers.

Yet she had the frightened feeling that Walter would not respect the sanctity of God's House, but would be concerned only with gratifying her Stepmother and, of course, Sir Mortimer.

She was trembling as the Duke led her up the aisle, and she saw an old Clergyman ahead of them, moving along from the altar which was decorated with lilies.

The Duke walked until they were in front of the Parson, who intent on his thoughts, was only suddenly aware of them.

Raising his head he stared at them through his spectacles.

'I am sure, Vicar, that you are in a hurry to join the wedding-party,' the Duke said quietly, and drink the health of the bride. But if you will marry me to this young lady immediately, I will give two hundred pounds for the restoration of the Church!'

CHAPTER 6

For a second the Vicar stared at the Duke as if he thought he could not have heard aright. Then he said in a quavering voice:

'Did you—say two—hundred—pounds, Sir?'

'Two hundred,' the Duke repeated, 'and if you are in a hurry, so am I.'

He thought the Parson was hesitating, and he drew from his pocket a piece of paper which Valora, who was standing beside him too stunned to speak, realised was something she had seen before.

Almost as if the Parson had asked the question the Duke said:

'I have here a Special Licence, and let me give you the two hundred pounds immediately.'

He put his hands deep into his breeches pocket, which was where he had placed some of the notes of high denomination that Mr Dunham had given him.

He had hoped that if a Highwayman made him produce the sovereigns the notes underneath them would go undetected.

As the old Parson still stared at him as if mesmerised, the Duke placed the notes on top of the Special Licence, then with a smile he leant over the altar rails to put it on a table which was usually used for a Communion Plate.

As he did so, swiftly so neither the Parson nor Valora was aware of it, he transferred with his right hand his pistol from his riding-coat pocket into the waist of his breeches.

A Prayer Book was standing on the table and the Duke, having laid down the money and the Licence, picked it up and handed it to the Clergyman.

As if he was too surprised to make any protest, or it might have been the Duke's authoritative manner which swept away any questions he might have asked, the Parson opened the Prayer Book.

As he began the first prayer, the Duke heard quiet footsteps coming through the Church door and moving up a side aisle.

He knew it was the Highwayman, and thought with relief that whatever happened now, there were two of them to face the men in pursuit of Valora.

Then he knew he must concentrate on her, and that this was a very important moment in his own life.

He glanced at her, realised she was very pale, and that she was trembling.

At the same time she was behaving with a composure which he admired, because he was well aware how frightening it must be to know that at any moment she would be confronted by her Stepmother's servants.

The Vicar finished the prayer. Then as if he had suddenly remembered there was something he needed to know, he said:

'Please tell me your names.'

'Greville Alexander and Valora,' the Duke answered.

Then the Parson started the main part of the service:

'Wilt thou have this woman to thy wedded wife, to live together after God's ordinance in the Holy state of Matrimony? Wilt thou love her, comfort her, honour and keep her in sickness and in health; and forsaking all others keep thee only unto her, so long as ye both shall live?'

'I will.'

The Duke's voice had a depth and sincerity which made Valora feel it vibrate through her.

At the same time she was sure this was a dream, it could not really be happening. The fear that she might be captured and be taken back to Heverington was still like a knife in her heart.

At the same time something ecstatic was rising within her too, because the Duke was near her and she loved him! Yet she could not believe she was actually being married!'

Then the Vicar asked:

'*Valora, wilt thou have this man for your wedded husband, to live together after God's ordinance in the Holy state of Matrimony? Wilt thou love him, obey him, and serve him, honour and keep him in sickness and in health; and forsaking all others keep thee only unto him, so long as ye both shall live?*'

'I will.'

As Valora spoke she was sure the words were echoed by the voice of angels, and the Church was filled with Celestial music.

Then the Duke drew his signet ring from his little finger and took Valora's hand in his. Almost instinctively she swayed a little towards him so that their shoulders were touching.

'*With this Ring I thee Wed,*' he said in his deep voice. '*With my body I thee worship, and with all my worldly goods I thee endow...*'

He slipped the ring onto her finger.

She looked up at him as he did so, and thought there was an expression in his eyes that she had never seen before.

The Vicar told them to kneel and, when they did so, he raised his hand and blessed them.

Again it seemed to Valora as if a paean of music from the spheres filled the Church, and the Blessing came not from one frail old man, but from God Himself.

Then as the Blessing finished the Duke raised Valora to her feet.

He was wondering whether she would be frightened if he kissed her.

Then as he looked down into her eyes, there was a sudden noise of the Church door being pushed violently open and a clump of heavy footsteps.

As Valora gave a little cry of fear, the Duke turned round to face the two men who had been pursuing them.

As they came stamping up the aisle, he recognised the man he had seen in the Dining Hall on the first night of his journey, and knew him to be Walter.

He was a dark, swarthy individual, with shifty eyes, and a tight-lipped, cruel mouth.

The other man, Giles, was fair and somewhat nondescript, but like Walter he held a pistol in his hand.

They walked halfway up the aisle before they

stopped and faced the Duke and Valora, who were standing in front of the Altar. The clergyman behind them was a step higher than they were.

For a moment no one spoke, and then Walter said in an ugly voice:

'You've given us a good run, Miss Valora, but now we've got you.'

'You are too late,' the Duke replied quietly but distinctly. ' "Miss Valora", as you call her is now my wife.'

'That's what I suspected might be happening when I hears you were in here,' Walter answered, 'but a bridegroom's no good to a woman if he's dead.'

As he spoke he lowered the pistol in his hand slightly to bring it down on to the Duke, pointing it at his heart.

As he did so the Highwayman, who had concealed himself behind a pillar, shot him dead!

Walter's finger had been on the trigger, and as he staggered backwards his pistol went off, the bullet passing harmlessly over the top of the Altar.

The Duke, however, was not watching Walter fall but Giles, and after one indecisive moment as Walter collapsed at his side, his finger tightened on the trigger.

With the quickness of a man who had lived with danger, the Duke shot him a split second before the bullet from Giles's pistol would have hit him.

This time as the servant's gun exploded the bullet hit the lectern at exactly the height, had the aim not been deflected, to strike the Duke's head.

The noise of the pistol-shots and the suddenness with which everything occurred had left not only Valora but also the Vicar paralysed with horror.

Only as the Highwayman came from behind the pillar did the old man say:

'What—is happening?—I do not—understand. Who are these—men?'

'It is quite all right, Vicar,' the Duke replied soothingly. 'They are Highwaymen and as such are better dead, rather than preying on innocent people.'

'Highwaymen!' the Vicar murmured. 'Then they are indeed wicked creatures! But that such killing should happen in Church is not right—no indeed, it is not right at all.'

'I agree,' the Duke replied. 'And if you will take my wife into the Vestry my friend and I will remove their bodies from this sacred place.'

He smiled at Valora reassuringly as he spoke,

and once again he was proud of the way she moved towards the old Vicar to help him down the Chancel steps and support him as they walked together into the Vestry.

"Another woman," the Duke thought, "would be screaming and crying at being involved in anything so dramatic and unpleasant."

He thought as he watched her move away that he loved her with an intensity that he found it hard to express even to himself.

Then, as there were more immediate things for him to think about, he walked to where the Highwayman was standing looking down at the dead bodies of their opponents.

The blood had flowed from the wounds in their chests, and the Duke thought the Highwayman's prophecy had certainly come true.

'What do you intend to do with them?' William Travers asked.

'Put them in the porch and tell the Vicar to inform the Magistrates, who will have them collected.'

'Do you really think anyone will believe they are really Highwaymen?'

'Why not?' the Duke replied. 'Have you anything on you which would identify you as William Travers?'

The Highwayman looked at him in surprise. Then as he understood what the Duke was planning, there was a sudden light in his eyes.

'I have a book I always carry with me,' he answered. 'The Teachings of St Augustine.'

'Your name is inscribed in it?'

'Yes, indeed! It was given me by my godfather when I was confirmed.'

As he spoke he took a small leather-bound book from the pocket of his coat, and the Duke saw written on the inside cover in a firm hand the words:

'To William Travers on the day of his confirmation at St Albans Abbey. April 23rd 1804.'

The Duke nodded, then looked first at Mr Travers then at Giles. In type the two were not unlike; as both were fair, both thin and clean-shaven.

'Empty his pockets of everything except money,' the Duke ordered.

The Highwayman obeyed. Then he slipped into the dead man's pocket the book which contained his name.

As he stood up and straightened his back there was a light in his eyes which had not been there before.

The Duke was looking to see what Walter carried in his coat. He drew out a notebook, an account for the monies they had spent on the journey and two letters and put them all into his own pocket.

Then he turned to pull the dead man by his coat collar down the aisle and out into the porch. He flung him down on the flagstones and following him William Travers did the same thing with Giles.

'They deserved to die,' he said as if he was excusing his own conscience for the killing.

'From what you have told me, there is no doubt about that,' the Duke answered, 'and now you can start a new life. How you can do so is written in a letter I was waiting to give you when we next met.'

He drew, as he spoke, a note from inside his coat and handed it to the Highwayman, who looked down at it with a questioning expression on his face. The Duke understood what he was thinking without the need to put it into words.

'If you imagine it is money,' he said, 'you are mistaken.'

Because that was exactly what he had been expecting, William Travers raised his eyes.

'It concerns your future,' the Duke said, 'And a suggestion of employment which I feel would be of considerable interest to you.'

William Travers drew in a deep breath.

'There is only one condition attached to it,' the Duke went on. 'You must promise not to open it until you think I have reached York.'

Before he could reply the Duke asked:

'How long might that be? I have no idea exactly where I am?'

'You are now a little north of Doncaster,' Travers replied, 'and you can reach York in three hours if you ride hard.'

The Duke smiled.

'Then that is what we will do. So in three hours time—no, better make it four for safety—you can open that letter. I shall be very disappointed if you are not pleased with what you read.'

'You are making me unbearably curious,' William Travers said in a low voice. 'But I have a feeling that I shall want to thank you from the very bottom of my heart.'

'You will be able to do that in the future if you agree to what I suggest,' the Duke answered. 'But please observe the condition I have made. You will realise its importance when I tell you a wager depends on it.'

He spoke with a mocking note in his voice and William Travers laughed.

'After all we have been through together,' he

said, 'I can appreciate the importance really lies in the fact that it is very different from death and damnation.'

'That describes the events of the last few minutes very eloquently,' the Duke replied, 'but you realise it is vitally important that from this moment William Travers, the Highwayman with a price on his head, is a dead man.'

He spoke seriously and gave a brief glance at Giles lying at their feet.

'I can only say "thank you",' William Travers said in a voice that vibrated with sincerity.

'I did not forsee what has actually happened,' the Duke went on, 'but I was aware that it would be a tragedy and a shocking waste of your abilities for you to continue being hounded by the Military, and unable to work while there was a price on your head.'

William Travers looked at him excitedly as the Duke continued:

'I therefore took the liberty of re-naming you, and as I always think it is wise to keep as near as possible to the truth I have called you William Thornton.'

'I have always understood it is a godfather's privilege to name the child,' his companion replied with a touch of laughter in his voice.

'I am glad you approve,' the Duke said, 'and now from this moment you must forget everything but your new identity.'

He held out his hand as he spoke.

'While I shall not forget, Thornton, that you saved my life.'

The two men clasped hands and the new William Thornton replied:

'I shall always remember that you have given me a new life.'

'I hope you will enjoy it,' the Duke answered, 'and now my wife and I must be on our way.'

He walked back into the Church and went into the Vestry where he found Valora waiting on a chair beside the Vicar.

She looked up as the Duke came in through the door, and he saw by the light in her eyes how glad she was to see him.

'We must leave,' he said quietly, 'but first I want to thank the Vicar for marrying us, and apologise for keeping him so long from the bridal party.'

'He is rather...upset by what has...occurred,' Valora said in a low voice.

'Of course he is,' the Duke replied, 'but I think, Sir, you have behaved with courage and dignity that is embellishment to the office you hold.'

The old man flushed at the Duke's praise and rose to his feet.

'I am sure you are right, Sir,' he said, 'in thinking the world is a better place without those Highwaymen. At the same time they should not have come into the sanctity of my Church carrying firearms.'

'It is something they will never do again,' the Duke replied lightly. 'Now if you will excuse us, my wife and I have to reach York before it grows too late.'

'Then you must leave at once,' the Vicar answered instantly. 'It is a long way, but I expect you have good horses to convey you there.'

'We have indeed,' the Duke answered, 'but may I suggest we leave by a different door, and that you get someone later to collect what is blocking the usual entrance to the Church.'

The Vicar understood and held out his hand to Valora.

'Goodbye my child,' he said. 'May I wish you two young people every happiness and a long life together. I feel although what has happened at your wedding may have spoilt it for you, that God has given you his Blessing.'

'I am sure He has,' Valora replied in a low voice, 'and thank you for your kindness.'

She curtsied and the Vicar shook hands with

the Duke.

'Look after her,' he said. 'You are a very lucky man to have such a charming wife.'

'Very lucky,' the Duke agreed.

The Vicar let them out by the Vestry door, and they walked round the Church to the lych-gate, where William Thornton was waiting beside the horses. The Duke lifted Valora on to the saddle and said:

'Say goodbye to our friend, he is going South and we are going North. But we are both aware it is due to him that I am—alive—.'

'...and I am not being taken back to Heverington,' Valora said almost beneath her breath.'

She bent towards William Thornton with her hand outstretched.

'Thank you...thank you,' she said. 'If you had not been able to warn us...they might have taken us...unawares.'

There was a distinct tremor in her voice as she spoke.

'It is all over now,' he replied, 'and they will never trouble you again. Nor will anyone else—your husband will see to that.'

'We shall see you again sometime?' Valora asked.

'Your husband has plans for me. I am very content to be in his hands.'

William Thornton glanced at the Duke as he spoke, and the two men smiled at each other. Then he lifted Valora's hand to his lips and said:

'I feel sure, Miss Valora—it is difficult to think of you as anything else—you will be very happy.'

The Duke started to move away on Samson.

'I hope so,' Valora replied.

She wanted to ask him how she could keep in touch but she thought it was a stupid question. How could a Highwayman have an address. Then it struck her she had no idea what her own address would be.

As if the spell which had enveloped her ever since she entered the church suddenly lifted, Valora became vividly aware that she was married, she had a husband, and she knew nothing about him.

Her heart was singing because she was free of the fear that had been with her day and night, ever since her Stepmother had told her she was to marry Sir Mortimer.

It was a fear that had overshadowed her thoughts and feelings from the moment she woke to the moment she went to sleep.

Even in her dreams he had been pursuing her, and she had known instinctively that he was everything that was bad, cruel and evil, and only a miracle could save her from becoming his wife.

The miracle had occurred in the shape of a man who had been occupying the bedroom next door, and when Walter, who she felt was an instrument of the Devil, was only ten minutes behind them, this stranger had saved her again...saved her for all time!

Now she was free...free from her Stepmother and Sir Mortimer, and they had no jurisdiction over her.

But she was married!

The words seemed almost to be written in letters of fire in the sky as she rode after the Duke, trying to collect her thoughts, trying to believe that what had happened so swiftly and unexpectedly had actually taken place; and that she had become the wife of a man who had not even proposed to her.

As Mercury drew up alongside Samson, Valora glanced at the Duke from under her eyelashes, and thought there was a smile of satisfaction on his face.

He turned to look at her and she thought too there was a glint of triumph in his eyes.

Then without a word he started to ride fast and hard using the grass edge of the road and all the time heading North.

Now there were milestones, and the Duke saw when they passed the first one after the village that Thornton had been right in saying it would take them three hours to reach York.

He reckoned, therefore, they should be there before five o'clock, and he could not believe there would be more delays or hindrances on their way.

The horses, having had a rest while they had luncheon, responded to everything that was required of them.

Soon the traffic on the road increased; the country changed to become more undulating and more open, and the Duke thought they had entered the County of Yorkshire.

He was determined however not to have a conversation with Valora until she had recovered from the shock of seeing two men shot dead, and what he was sure had been little less of a shock at being married so unexpectedly.

At the same time he knew, with a feeling of happiness that he had never known before, that she was his and that however long it took he would eventually persuade her to love him as he loved her.

Without appearing to do so, he was watching her as she rode beside him, admiring the elegant manner in which she sat on her horse and the delicacy of her features under her gauzed-draped riding-hat.

"She is so sensitive and vulnerable," he thought, "that I must be very gentle with her until she grows used to me."

At the same time because he knew even to think of Valora made his blood quicken, it would be hard for him not to make love to her and to kiss her.

He felt his lips aching at the thought and he knew that every moment they were together he loved her more.

"She is everything I want as a wife," he told himself.

Once again he was commending the dignity and the composure she had shown in circumstances which would send most women into screaming hysterics.

It was almost inconceivable that everything should have played so fortunately into his hands.

If Walter and Giles had tracked them down to one of the Inns where they had stayed, the story might have indeed been very different, but the Duke thought that God had been on their side and good had undoubtedly triumphed over evil.

That was not the way he would have thought about it in the past, and he told himself that already Valora's purity was changing his outlook and his approach to problems whether they were large or small.

"I suppose Freddie will say I have found my soul," he thought to himself with a smile.

But it was not a mocking one as he knew he had not only found his soul—but Valora!

They reached the outskirts of York at about ten minutes to five and as the first building of the city came in sight, and Duke could see the tall tower of York Minster silhouetted against the sky.

He was aware that he had won his bet and that now he had to tell Valora who he actually was.

He was wondering what she would feel on learning he was not plain Mr Stanton, but a Duke!

As the horses slowed down because of the carriages, drays and carts on the road, he put out his hand to say:

'We are nearly there—you are not too tired?'

'Not in the least, only rather thirsty.'

'Now I think of it, so am I,' the Duke said.

Commonplace words, and yet he thought their eyes were saying very different things to each other. He told himself the sooner they arrived the better.

'Do you remember where your Grandfather lives?' he asked.

'Yes, of course,' Valora replied, 'in Bishopthorpe Palace.'

'Palace?' the Duke questioned.

'Oh...I forgot,' Valora said, '...perhaps I did not tell you, but Grandfather is the Archbishop of York.'

The Duke was astonished. He had expected Valora's grandfather to be just a country gentleman. Now it struck him that nothing could be more fortunate than that he should be the Archbishop of York.

He had already been thinking while they were riding of what his family's reaction to his marriage would be.

Although he knew they would all in time, come to love Valora for herself, he was aware that the more strait-laced of his female relatives would deplore that she should be the daughter of a man who had caused such a scandal by running away with the wife of an actor.

The Duke was prepared to defend Valora and prevent, if it was humanly possible, anyone from upsetting her.

But he was aware she was already sensitive

about such things because of the way she had been treated in the country and in London after her father died.

Now that he could lay stress on her relationship to an Archbishop, it would, he thought, smooth the way with those of his Aunts and Great Aunts who would be ready to condemn her however unfairly for her father's misdeeds.

'I am certainly looking forward to meeting your Grandfather,' he said out loud.

'I hope he will recognise me,' Valora replied. 'I have not seen him since I was twelve years old, and Mama took me to meet him in London when he came South for some special ceremony.'

'I expect you looked much as you do now,' the Duke answered lightly.

He turned his head to look at Valora, and then he was aware of someone waving frantically to him from the pavement.

As he drew in his horse in astonishment, Jenkins ran to his side.

'I knew Your Grace would do it!' he cried excitedly. 'Major Stanley said I were a fool to come and meet you, and you would be back in London while I was waiting here.'

'As you see Major Stanley was wrong,' the Duke replied. 'I am glad to see you Jenkins.'

He realised his Valet was looking in horror at his boots and the dust and stains on his white buckskin breeches.

Then it struck him Jenkins had addressed him as "Your Grace" and he turned to Valora to see her reaction to it.

But he saw she had not heard, because she was concerned with controlling Mercury from shying at a street vendor, who had a number of brightly coloured windmills on a handcart, and was carrying a number of balloons which were moving about in the wind.

The Duke bent from the saddle to say to Jenkins:

'I am still incognito, and you address me as "Sir".'

'Very good, Your—Sir.'

'We are going to Bishopthorpe Palace,' the Duke said. 'Follow us there. I presume you have a conveyance of some sort?'

'I came in the brake, Sir,' Jenkins grinned.

The Duke was amused, because he knew the brake when travelling long distances was pulled by six horses.

He could understand how Jenkins had managed to get ahead of them, especially as he had doubtless travelled directly up the main road and spent only a few hours a night sleeping.

Having asked the way, and learning that Bishopthorpe Palace lay South West of the City, they rode over open land until they saw the long flanking walls of the Gate house.

The Palace built on the banks of the River Ouse in the 15th century, had been rebuilt after the Restoration.

As they rode up to the front door the Duke was relieved to think that Jenkins was not far behind and he would not only be able to make a change of clothing but also enjoy a bath.

Then he realised as grooms appeared to take their horses that Valora was looking apprehensive.

As he lifted her down from the saddle the Duke said:

'Do not worry. If your Grandfather is not pleased to see us, there are plenty of other places we can go.'

'The hotels in York might be expensive,' she warned.

'That will be of no consequence,' the Duke replied, and thought she looked at him curiously.

The Butler who opened the door was an old man who seemed ready to say the Archbishop was not receiving guests.

'Will you tell...His Grace,' Valora said a little nervously, 'that it is his...granddaughter who has...called.'

The Butler stared at her.

'His granddaugher?' he repeated.

'My Mother was His Grace's daughter.'

'God Bless my soul!' the Butler declared. 'His Grace'll be delighted, really delighted Miss. He's often talked of Her Ladyship, and said how deeply he regretted not seeing her before she died.'

'She too would have liked to see him,' Valora said softly.

'Come this way, Miss, and I'll take you to His Grace. He is in the Library.'

The Butler led the way and as he went ahead Valora looked up at the Duke.

She put her hand into his and his fingers tightened reassuringly, and as he smiled at her she said a little prayer of gratefulness because he was there, and somehow nothing was frightening when he was beside her.

From the vaulted Gothic entrance hall the Butler opened the door of the Library where a man with white hair sat at the window as if he was enjoying the last rays of the sunshine before the sun sank.

The Butler crossed the room to stand beside,

him.

'A surprise, Your Grace, and a pleasant one! Her Ladyship's daughter's here. Your Grace'll remember we last saw her when you was in London.'

The Archbishop, who had been reading a book, raised his head, and the Duke saw he was a fine looking old man with a serene expression as if he had made his peace with God and man, and there were no troubles to mar the quietness of his eventide.

Valora moved forward.

'Do you remember me, Grandpapa?' she asked. 'It is a long time since I last saw you.'

'It is indeed Valora,' the Archbishop replied, 'but you are very like your mother.'

'I am glad you think so,' Valora said. 'She used to speak of you with great love and was always so sad she was not well enough to come North and visit you.'

'I always remember her in my prayers,' the Archbishop said gently, 'and you, my child.'

'Thank you,' Valora replied.

She bent forward and kissed her Grandfather on the cheek, then looked round at the Duke. Before she could speak the Archbishop enquired:

'And who is this you have brought with you?'

The Duke held out his hand.

'I am the Duke of Brockenhurst, Your Grace. Valora and I were married this afternoon.'

'Married!' the Archbishop exclaimed. 'But where, and why was I not told?'

The Duke hardly heard what the old man said because he was looking at Valora.

He saw the astonishment in her face as she heard his words, and he was sure she was not only surprised but a little frightened.

'A lot of things have happened, Your Grace, which we would like to relate to you in detail,' the Duke said to the Archbishop, 'but may I suggest something first?'

'Yes, of course,' the Archbishop replied.

'If it is possible, we would like to stay here with you tonight.'

'But naturally you must stay,' the Archbishop answered.

He looked to where the Butler was still hovering by the door.

'Bates, have rooms for my Granddaughter and her husband prepared and tell Cook they will be here for dinner.'

'I'll do that, Your Grace,' Bates said with satisfaction, 'and everyone in the house'll be delighted.'

'My Valet is just behind us with my luggage,'

the Duke remarked as the Butler went from the room.

Then he turned back to the Archbishop.

'There is something else I would like to ask Your Grace.'

'And what is that?'

'Your Granddaughter and I had a very strange kind of marriage this afternoon. It was something that was expedient at the time, but it was not the sort of wedding that we will want to remember in the years ahead. Nor did Valora have the permission of a Guardian. Would it be possible for Your Grace to marry us again?'

As the Duke finished speaking he heard Valora give a little gasp. Then before her Grandfather could reply she cried:

'Oh, please Grandpapa, it would be very... very wonderful if you could marry us...properly.'

The Archbishop smiled.

'But of course, my children, nothing would give me greater pleasure.'

As the Archbishop spoke Valora felt the excitement of it must be shared and she put out her hand towards the Duke.

He took it in his and because he sensed the happiness behind such an impulsive gesture he almost squeezed the blood from her fingers.

'Now I am sure you would like to go to your rooms,' the Archbishop said. 'By the time you have unpacked and changed my Chaplain will have arranged for the ceremony to take place here in my private Chapel.'

He paused before he went on:

'You will understand that at my age I go to bed very early before dinner, so if you could be ready in perhaps an hour and a half, that would be the easiest from my point of view.'

'But of course we will be ready, Grandpapa,' Valora said, 'and thank you for agreeing to marry us. I know how happy it would make Mama.'

The Archbishop touched her shoulder affectionately, and with the other hand he rang the small bell that stood beside him. The door opened immediately and Bates the Butler said in a tone of satisfaction.

'Everything is arranged, Your Grace, and the luggage is just being carried upstairs.'

Valora did not understand, but only as they followed the Butler upstairs and saw ahead of them two footmen carrying a large trunk did she look at the Duke questioningly.

'My Valet came from London to meet me,' he explained. 'He spoke to me while you were having a little trouble with Mercury and some extremely buoyant balloons.'

Valora laughed.

'Mercury hates things that float about in the air. If he had not been so tired he would have protested more violently than he did.'

'I am sure he will enjoy being in a really comfortable stable for the first time in several nights.'

As he spoke the Duke looked with satisfaction at the large bedroom into which they were being shown by a Housekeeper in rustling black silk.

'May I welcome Your Grace,' she said as she curtsied to Valora. 'I knew your mother when she was a small girl, and it's a real pleasure to have Your Grace with us.'

'Thank you,' Valora replied.

She spoke shyly, the Duke knew, because she had been addressed for the first time as a Duchess.

Then as the Housekeeper showed Valora the bedroom with its painted ceiling and large bed with gilt posts to support a carved canopy, Bates took the Duke to the room next door where Jenkins was waiting.

The two footmen were undoing his trunks and his gold hair brushes already adorned the dressing-table.

Valora however was looking rather forlornly at the small bundle that had been brought upstairs from Mercury's saddle.

She thought it was the most marvellous idea she had ever heard when the Duke had suggested her Grandfather should marry them again.

He had been right when he said she did not want to think of their marriage-service ending with two men being shot in the aisle of the Church.

But now, womanlike, she wanted to look the part of the bride.

As if the Housekeeper, whose name was Mrs Field, followed her thoughts, she said:

'Is that all the luggage you have with you, Your Grace, or have they placed a trunk in the wrong room?'

'No,' Valora replied, 'the only gown I have with me had to be carried on the back of my horse's saddle.'

She managed a brave little smile as she added:

'I am afraid it is rather the worse for wear.'

As she spoke the Housekeepr was already undoing the bundle, and she pulled out the white gown which Valora thought mournfully would certainly not appear very spectacular.

'Oh dear!' she exclaimed. 'I wish I had

something prettier to wear for my wedding!'

The Housekeeper looked at her in a puzzled way and Valora explained:

'I was married this afternoon but it was a very hurried ceremony in a village Church, and my...my...husband has asked Grandpapa if he will marry us again as soon as we have washed and changed.'

She paused and added sadly:

'That is all I have to change into.'

'Well, Your Grace, there is certainly something we can do about that,' Mrs Field replied.

Valora looked at the Housekeeper as if the darkness of the sky had suddenly opened and there was an unexpected ray of sunshine.

'Are you saying...are you suggesting that you might have a...gown for me?' she asked breathlessly.

'If it's a wedding-gown you're wanting, Your Grace,' Mrs Field replied. 'I've not one but two!'

'But how...what do you...mean?' Valora enquired.

Mrs Field gave a respectful little laugh.

'Your Mother, Your Grace, took her wedding-gown away with her, but your Grandmama's dress is still here, and so is your Great-Grandmother's.'

'Wedding-dresses...there are wedding dresses!' Valora exclaimed. 'Do you really think they would fit me...and I can wear one?'

'You leave everything to me, Your Grace,' Mrs Field said briskly. 'Get undressed and have a bath, which the maids have prepared through here.'

She opened the door on the other side of the room, and Valora saw to her surprise it led into a bathroom built, she thought, into what had originally been thirty years earlier, a Powder Closet.

There was no running water, but huge brass cans filled with hot water had been provided from the kitchen and while she looked at the first one, a maid arrived with another can.

There was a delicious smell of flowers which Valora knew came from something which had been added to the water that was already in the bath.

Then as Mrs Field disappeared she went back into the bedroom and started to undress.

As she did so she knew that she wanted frantically to look attractive for the man she had married.

They had reached York, and he had not left her as she had expected him to. He was with her and though she could hardly believe it, he was a Duke.

But as she took off her riding-hat she knew that was unimportant. What really mattered was he had married her.

She was not certain whether he had done so, just because it was the only way he could save her from being taken back to Heverington Hall, or because he wanted her as his wife.

Then as she pulled off the rest of her clothes Valora was praying.

'Please God let him love me...Please God let him really want me as I know now I...want him.'

CHAPTER 7

Valora looked with delight at her reflection in the mirror.

She could hardly believe it could have happened that at a moment's notice she would find a wedding-gown that was the embodiment of all her romantic dreams.

Mrs Field produced the two gowns she had promised her but the moment Valora saw the one in which her Grandmother had been married in 1772 she knew that was the gown which would give her an appearance which she hoped the Duke would think enchanted.

Made of white satin trimmed with exquisite Brussels lace, the skirts were full but not so exaggerated as they had been later in the century.

The square neckline was cut low, revealing her white skin, and the sleeves were frilled over the elbows in a cascade of lace.

What made it so lovely, Valora thought, was that from the shoulders there was lace falling to the ground, and ending in a train several feet long.

Although it was old it had not yellowed with age, and when Mrs Field brought a lace veil to arrange over her hair Valora found it hard to find words in which to thank her.

There was a wreath of orange blossom which Mrs Field said was particularly lucky because not only her Grandmother had worn it, but also her mother.

'I wish she was here today,' Valora murmured, speaking really to herself, but Mrs Field heard her.

'I'm sure she is, Your Grace,' she said. 'We who believe in the afterlife—and who could believe in anything else with your Grandfather as near a Saint as anyone on earth—know that those we love are always near us.'

'Thank you...for reminding...me,' Valora said softly, and blinked away the tears that filled her eyes.

Then she glanced at the clock on the mantelpiece and realised that there was still ten minutes before her Grandfather would be waiting for them.

She had a sudden thought that had not occurred to her previously and she said to Mrs Field:

'I would like to speak to my...my...my husband. Do you think...he has gone...downstairs?'

'In that case I'll send someone to fetch him, Your Grace,' Mrs Field replied.

'No...I would not...wish...' Valora started to say, but it was too late.

Mrs Field had already left the room and she stood indecisive, wondering if she should say what was in her mind, or let the arrangements the Duke had made with her Grandfather go ahead.

That he had married her was the most marvellous thing that had ever happened, and she had felt as they knelt in front of the altar in the village Church, there were angels' voices in the air above them and they were receiving the Blessing of God.

All the same, she knew now they had not only been married with a Special Licence which had not belonged to them, but the Duke had not given his full name and, as he had said himself, though under-age, she had not the permission of her Guardian.

"It was not a legal marriage," Valora thought, "and I must set him...free if...that is what he...wants."

She thought to do so would tear her heart from her body, but what was the point of marrying a man who did not really want her?

He had only saved her out of kindness as he

had saved her once before?

'I love him!' Valora whispered.

She felt as if the words throbbed through her whole body despairingly, almost as if she said "goodbye" to something that was so perfect, so beautiful, that it was as elusive as the sunshine, and it would never really have been hers.

She heard a footstep outside the door and as the handle turned she felt herself trembling.

The Duke came into the room and for a moment Valora hardly recognised him.

He was dressed in the height of fashion and she drew in her breath at the magnificence of him in his satin knee breeches, black silk stockings, and long-tailed coat with several diamond decorations.

His high cravat, tied in an intricate, complicated style seemed to give him a new dignity, while at the same time with the knots above his chin it accentuated his handsome looks.

As if he understood why she was staring at him with wide eyes, the Duke smiled as he shut the door behind him and came towards her.

'If you are surprised by my appearance,' he said gently, 'may I tell you that you look very lovely, and exactly the bride I always hoped to marry.'

Valora drew in her breath. Then she said

quickly, before she might find it impossible to say the words:

'I...I want to...speak to you about...our...m-marriage.'

There was a little tremor in her voice which the Duke did not miss, and he replied:

'I am listening to anything you wish to say.'

He was aware that she was perturbed, and he saw too that her fingers were trembling.

'We are already married,' he said soothingly, 'in very frightening circumstances, but now there is nothing to make you afraid.'

'That is...not what I want to...say to you.'

The Duke did not speak, and after a moment Valora went on:

'I realised when you told Grandpapa that we had been...married without the...permission of my Guardian that it was illegal. I think...therefore...if you wish it that it...could be cancelled...or annulled...I do not know...what the right word is.'

She could not look at the Duke as she spoke, afraid she might see an expression of relief in his eyes.

As her voice trembled into silence Valora felt he must hear the beating of her heart.

'Is that what you want?' he asked quietly.

She wanted to cry out that it was not only

what she did not want, but what she dreaded and feared, that she might lose him and never see him again.

Yet because she felt she must give him the chance to escape that he had given her, she said in a voice he could hardly hear:

'I...I thought...perhaps you would want to be...free now that you have s-saved me...and I shall be...safe with Grandpapa.'

'You are thinking only of me?'

'Y-yes. It is...only right that I should...do so.'

'And what about yourself? Do you want to be free?'

He saw her clench her fingers together. Then because she knew he was waiting for a reply to his question, she managed to say:

'I...I want you to be...h-happy.'

'And if I tell you that I am very happy as things are at the moment?'

'But you are a...Duke,' Valora persisted. 'There must be many...women you would... rather marry than...me.'

'I have never asked any woman to marry me, Valora, nor, as it happens, did I ask you.'

There was a smile on the Duke's lips as he spoke and Valora answered:

'There was no time to do so and it was very clever...very wonderful of you to decide so quickly that was how you could...save me. But it nearly resulted in your...death.'

'If I had died, would you have minded?'

Valora gave a little cry of sheer horror.

'How can you ask me such a question? I thought when I saw those pistols pointing at you that you would...die and I knew that...'

She stopped suddenly, feeling that what she had been about to say was too revealing.

The Duke came nearer to her and took one of her hands in his.

'There is no need for you to finish that sentence,' he said, 'and I intend, Valora, to return to this conversation after we are married. Now your Grandfather is waiting for us in the Chapel, and as he is an old man I think we should be on time.'

He spoke firmly, but because he was touching her Valora felt as if her heart turned several somersaults and it was impossible to think of anything but that he was close to her and she loved him.

She looked up and her eyes met his.

Then somehow words were entirely superfluous and she knew that he wanted her as she wanted him, and they belonged to each other.

The Duke released her hand and offered her his arm.

'Come, my darling,' he said.

She felt as if they were suddenly enveloped in a celestial light and her heart was singing with happiness, as he led her towards the door.

★ ★ ★ ★

Walking back from the Chapel, Valora could see through the window where the curtains had not yet been drawn that the sun was sinking in a blaze of glory, and she felt as if the beauty of it filled her heart and mind.

The service in the little Chapel had been a very short one because, as her Grandfather's Chaplain who had escorted them there had explained, the Archbishop had not been well and on his doctor's advice took very few services these days.

But while he had been assisted by his Chaplain and another parson it was, Valora thought, her Grandfather's voice that made the words of the ceremony seem so sacred and so moving.

She had thought when they were married earlier in the day because she loved the Duke she had, as she repeated her vows, said them with a sincerity that seemed to come from her heart.

Now she felt as if her very soul was joined spiritually with the Duke's not only in this life, but for all eternity.

Her Grandfather blessed the ring before the Duke put it on her finger, and she saw that it was not the signet-ring with which he had married her previously but a gold wedding-ring which she learned later had belonged to her Grandmother.

When it encircled her finger she knew that he was making her his, and she would not only love and obey him, but adore and even worship him because he had lifted her from the depths of despair into a happiness that was not of this world.

They looked at each other and she thanked God passionately in her heart for giving her the love of a man who was so outstanding and very wonderful in every way.

It was not simply that he was a Duke and of great social importance, but because he was brave, resourceful, kind and considerate.

He had helped her because she was suffering and, as he had said himself, he could not "pass by on the other side".

They walked in silence towards the Drawing-Room and only when they reached it did the Duke say with a smile:

'Two weddings in one day! It is not many women who can boast of that!'

'I shall certainly want to boast about it,' Valora answered. 'But I have always heard that men hate weddings, so perhaps you would have preferred only one, and a very normal one at that!'

'What I have always dreaded, apart from being married,' the Duke said, 'was the thought of facing a huge congregation of my friends, ushers and bridesmaids and a wedding-breakfast at which people invariably make the most inane speeches in extremely bad taste!'

Valora laughed as he had intended her to do, and the Duke said:

'Now I suggest we have something to eat because I have a feeling it is a very long time since we lingered by that enchanted stream.'

'How could we have guessed when we...left it what was going to...happen?' Valora asked.

'I suppose we might say,' the Duke replied, 'that it was fate that Mercury should cast a shoe, fate that a wedding was taking place in the village Church, and fate that Walter should have found us at exactly the right moment, when Thornton and I could deal with him.'

'Thornton?' Valora questioned. 'Surely you mean Travers?'

'That is another of today's surprises,' the Duke said. 'Shall I tell you about him at dinner?'

The Butler offered the glasses of champagne and as they sipped the golden wine announced that dinner was served.

Once again the Duke offered Valora his arm and they walked down a different passage until a footman opened the door of the Dining-Room.

Valora saw a table lit with golden candelabra waiting for them, and she asked:

'What about Grandpapa? Should we not say goodnight to him?'

'He told me before he went to the Chapel,' the Duke answered, 'that he wished to spend a little time praying for our happiness, and then retire. He said he would see you in the morning.'

'I understand,' Valora replied.

She moved ahead of the Duke towards the table, conscious as she did so, that the whole room was a setting for them both—for her in her exquisite gown, still wearing her wreath and veil, the Duke looking as if he had just come from attendance on the King.

As if by right he sat in the high-backed chair at the top of the table with the Ecclesiastical arms which was usually occupied by her Grandfather.

The table was decorated with white flowers and the servants brought them delicious food on priceless silver dishes that were part of the treasure owned by successive Archbishops.

But Valora was only conscious of the Duke. For the first time in his presence she felt shy, and it was not so easy to talk to him in the academic fashion in which they had argued on their journey.

Now she was acutely conscious of the look in his eyes that she had never seen there before, and a caressing note in his voice that made her feel she wanted to touch him.

When the servants withdrew the Duke sat back, a glass of brandy beside him and she thought how different this meal had been from those they had eaten in the country Inns at which they had stayed on their wild dash to York.

As if once again he read her thoughts the Duke said:

'You and I were victorious, which I always felt in my heart we would be!'

'I wanted to think that too,' Valora said, 'but I was afraid of being over confident.'

'Is it necessary for me to tell you how splendid you were?' the Duke asked. 'I had no idea any woman could be so brave or so controlled.'

She knew he was thinking of that terrifying moment in the Church when Walter had fallen dead from the Highwayman's bullet, and when the Duke had saved himself from death by a split second.

'That is a moment I think we both want to forget,' he said quietly, 'except that one day it will be a splendid tale to tell our children and our grandchildren.'

As he spoke he watched the colour rise in Valora's cheeks and thought it was like the dawn lighting up the darkness of the world and was the loveliest thing he had ever seen.

'It served its purpose,' he went on, 'and like spring following the darkness of winter it gave our friend and benefactor, William Travers, a new life.'

'You called him "Thornton" just now,' Valora said in a puzzled voice.

'That is something I want to explain to you,' the Duke replied.

He told her in a few words how he had made the Highwayman empty Giles' pockets and replace them with the book which bore his name.

'When the two bodies are taken from the

porch and examined,' he went on, 'there will be no reason for anyone to suspect their identity.'

'It was clever, so very clever!' Valora gasped.

'What is more,' the Duke said in a tone of satisfaction, 'it is unlikely that anyone will connect the wedding that took place ostensibly between the Honourable George Hughes and Charlotte Mayhem with ours.'

He put his hand over Valora's as he said:

'That is another reason why I wished your Grandfather to marry us, although the first and most important one was that there could be no possible question of your not being my legal wife.'

'You...really want...me?' Valora asked breathlessly.

'In a very short while I intend to tell you how much,' the Duke answered, 'but I do not wish you to remain curious about our friend—William Thornton.'

'You said he was going South.'

'I have sent him to Hurst Castle,' the Duke said, 'your future home, my precious, with instructions to my Agent that he shall set up Schools, if they are not already there, for the children of my employees. He will be in complete charge, and, if necessary, engage more teachers.'

Valora gave a little cry.

'How could you do anything so marvellous? Nothing, nothing...could make me happier, or please me more!'

'That is what I thought you would say,' the Duke said, 'and when Thornton has completed his task at the Castle I have a number of other estates in other parts of the country where he can carry on his good work.'

Valora clasped her hands together.

'He will be so happy,' she said, 'and you could not have rewarded him in a better, or more practical fashion.'

'That is what I thought,' the Duke agreed, 'and as William Travers is dead, I think perhaps with your and my help William Thornton will become very much in demand as an advisor, because I am certain I can get a number of my friends to follow my example.'

Valora looked at him with so much gratitude and happiness that her eyes seemed brighter than the light from the candles.

The Duke smiled.

'You once said to me that knowledge was like looking up and trying to count the stars.'

'You remember I said that!' Valora exclaimed.

'I remember everything you have said to me,' the Duke replied. 'Now I want you in the future to help me count the stars in a different way.'

Valora looked puzzled and he explained:

'You have so much to teach me, my darling, so much knowledge to impart to me of things which I have never thought about until now.'

'I wish...that was...true.'

'It is true!' the Duke insisted. 'You see everything that happens in a way that is different from other women. You make the simplest things in life seem beautiful and exciting, you show kindness and understanding to people who until now had never come into my life, nor have I been aware of their problems.'

As the Duke spoke he thought how pleased Freddie would have been at what he was saying, and he knew that he had not yet told Valora of the reason for his journey to York.

'If I could...help you in any...way,' she was saying. 'it would be very, very wonderful for me, but you are so wise, so clever, that I feel I shall never learn all the things I want you to... teach me.'

'There is one lesson,' the Duke said, 'which will thrill me more than anything else.'

'What is that?' Valora asked.

'I think you know the answer,' the Duke replied. 'It is love, my beautiful wife, and since from what you said to me when we sat by the stream I know that on that subject you are very ignorant, we will have to start from the very beginning.'

He waited for the colour to rise in her cheeks, and he thought the shyness in her eyes was so alluring, so lovely that the emotions she aroused in him made it hard to breathe.

Then as she did not speak, he said:

'I think we should go into the Drawing-Room.'

'Yes, of course,' Valora said quickly. 'Should I have retired...and left you to drink your brandy...alone?'

As if she felt she had made a social error she added quickly:

'I am afraid, because on other nights I have not done so, that you must think me ignorant in my social behaviour as well as in other ways.'

'I think you are utterly and completely adorable!' the Duke replied, 'but it is easier to talk without a table between us.'

Valora looked shy as she rose, and it was impossible for her eyes to meet the Duke's as they crossed the room to the door.

The walked slowly along the corridor hung

with portraits of previous occupants of the Palace, from Cardinal Wolsey and Kneller's picture of Archbishop Lamplugh.

When they reached the Drawing-Room with its delicious softly coloured Gothic ceiling, it was fragmented with the scent of flowers.

Although the candles were lit one window was left with the curtains parted and a French window was open into the garden.

Instinctively Valora crossed the room to stand at the open window looking out.

The sun had now sunk below the horizon, but there was still a translucent glow in the sky in which the first stars were coming out one by one.

She looked up at them and the Duke watched the graceful line of her neck and the exquisite straight line of her little nose against the darkness of the trees.

'Count the stars, my lovely,' he said very quietly, 'and when you tell me how many there are, I will tell you how many more there are to find.'

'You are laughing at me,' Valora accused, 'because I told you I was only interested in... knowledge and...nothing else was...important.'

'And now perhaps you have found you were wrong,' the Duke suggested.

'You...know I...have.'

'Will you tell me what you have found?'

As if she was suddenly conscious of the closeness of him, the insistent note in his words, and the enchantment which was sweeping over her, her voice seemed to have died in her throat.

And yet, because he was waiting she knew she had to answer him as if he had given her the command to do so.

'You are...making me...shy,' she whispered.

'I adore you when you are shy,' the Duke said. 'At the same time I want an answer to my question.'

'It is...difficult to say...because it is something you have...not said to...me.'

The Duke smiled as if he appreciated the way she was evading him, and he thought too that because she was elusive she attracted and enthralled him in a manner he had never known before.

'I think you have forgotten,' he said, 'that twice today you promised to obey me.'

'I have...not forgotten,' Valora replied, 'and...you also made some very...special vows...'

'Shall I say them for the third time?' the Duke enquired.

His question made her turn her eyes from the stars to look at him, and he said very softly:

' "To have and to hold from this day forward," and that is what I mean to do, Valora!'

As he spoke he put his arms around her and drew her close to him, and as he did so he felt a quiver that went through her and he knew that he too was quivering because she was so soft and sweet and he had controlled himself for so long.

Then he remembered how brave she had been and how, although it seemed a long time, it was only a day or so ago that she told him she would never marry.

He thought she had changed her mind, but he had to be certain and while he drew her still closer to him he did not kiss her, but instead he said:

'Listen to me, my precious little wife, I have something of importance to say to you.'

'What...is it?' Valora asked.

There was a sudden note of fear in her voice as if she thought something had gone wrong.

'It is nothing frightening,' the Duke said, 'it is just because I love you and because I want your happiness more than I have ever wanted anything for myself.'

He paused before he went on:

'I am aware that everything that has happened has been unprecedentedly hasty. It was something which neither of us could have avoided, and once again you can attribute it, if you like, to fate.'

He was aware that Valora had stiffened in his arms while she was listening.

'What I am trying to say,' he continued, 'is that if you wish to wait a little while until we know each other better before I make love to you, as I wish to do, before I teach you the lesson that is more important than any other to us both, then I will agree, and we will go on being friends until you are ready for me.'

When he had finished speaking he felt the tenseness go out of Valora's body, although that was difficult as they were so close already.

He waited. Then she said in a very low voice he could hardly hear:

'I...understand what you are...saying to me... and now I can answer your question...I love... you!'

The Duke put his fingers under Valora's chin and turned her face up to his.

'Do you mean that?'

'I love you!' Valora repeated, 'and I have been afraid...so desperately afraid...that when we reached here you would...leave me and I would never...see you again.'

The pain the words evoked was very obvious.

'My precious!' the Duke murmured.

'I love you...I love you!' Valora said again. 'Please teach...me about love...because I want to make you love...me.'

'I do that already,' the Duke said. 'And my lovely darling, how can I be so fortunate as to have found you?'

As he spoke his mouth found Valora'a and there was no further need for words.

Her lips were just as he had thought they would be: soft, sweet, innocent and unsure, and he knew it was what he had been seeking all his life, although he had not been aware of it.

Then as he realised she was not afraid and he felt they were joined spiritually as well as physically by a rapture that seeped through them both, his kisses became more demanding.

Time stood still and for Valora it was as if the stars had fallen from the sky to envelop them both in a light that was part of her heart and her mind.

'I love you! I love you!' she wanted to say over and over again, and she knew that all the knowledge she ever needed lay in the Duke's arms, his lips and in him.

When he finally raised his head she was trembling with the wonder of it and she felt that he was too.

'My wife! Mine!' he exclaimed as if they were the only words which he could express his feelings.

★ ★ ★ ★

A long time later, when they lay in the big four-poster bed, Valora realised that the Duke had pulled the curtains so that they could see the stars shining in what was now the darkness of the sky.

She moved a little closer to him and he asked with an inexpressible tenderness in his voice:

'Are you happy, my precious one?'

'I am so...happy,' Valora answered, 'that I think I am no...longer on earth, but one of the... stars which we can see out...there.'

'That is what I feel too,' the Duke said, 'and we are there together, my darling, and that is the only thing that matters.'

Valora lifted her face towards his.

'I was thinking,' she said, 'how foolish you must have thought me when I told you I would...never fall...in love and had no wish to be...married.'

'I was just as foolish myself,' the Duke replied. 'I had no wish to be married because I thought it would be impossible to find a woman who would not bore me and with whom I would not feel restricted or imprisoned.'

'Supposing...I bore you...in time?'

'That would be impossible,' he answered, 'first because we still have a thousand subjects to discuss, argue about, and secondly, because I have never before met anybody who inspired me to change my way of life.'

He kissed her hair before he went on:

'You have found me important things to do; things which will take up a great deal of our time.'

'Have I...really done...that?'

'Beginning with our protegee, William Thornton,' the Duke said. 'I am certain both you and he will want me to take up the cause of education for the masses in the House of Lords, and from what I know of it already, which is little, it is a subject which will mean a hard fight and a campaign in which we shall need not only to use our intelligence, but recruit a great number of other people to support us.'

'It would be a wonderful thing to do!' Valora cried. 'At the same time I am still afraid that because I am so...ignorant on the...subject of...love you may find somebody much more... experienced to...amuse you.'

The Duke looked back over the years and

knew he had found a great number of women who were sophisticated and experienced but who had always left him dissatisfied and eventually no longer interested.

With Valora it was different and he said:

'You have forgotten one thing—we agreed that human beings have to find the other part of themselves, and I am completely and absolutely convinced that I have found mine.'

Valora gave a cry of happiness.

'How can...I be sure of...that?' she asked.

'By loving me,' the Duke answered.

He turned so that he could hold her closer still and his lips moved first over the softness of her forehead, then he kissed her eyes.

'I adore you!' he said. 'You excite me so madly, my darling, that I am afraid it is you who will grow bored with me.'

'I will never do that,' Valora answered, 'because I know now how wrong I was when I said I did not want...love. It is the most wonderful...perfect...sacred thing that could happen to...anyone!'

She spoke in a passionate little voice which brought a hint of fire to the Duke's eyes, then unexpectedly she hid her face against him and said in a whisper:

'Now you have...taught me...how a woman...

starts a baby I know that it is the most glorious and beautiful star of the...night.'

'That is how I want you to think,' the Duke said, 'and, my precious, if that is what you now believe, I am satisfied that I am a very successful teacher.'

'You are marvellous, wonderful, magnificent!' Valora cried, 'I love you until I cannot think or feel or dream of anything but...love which of course is...you!'

'We will count the stars together,' the Duke said.

Then his heart was beating against hers, and there was no need to count the stars for they were with them in the light of love which is the knowledge of God.

Magna Print Books hope you have enjoyed this Large Print book. All our Large Print titles are designed for the easiest reading, and all our books are made to last. Other Magna Large Print Books are available at your library, through selected book-stores, or direct from the publisher. For more information about our current and forth-coming Large Print titles, please send your name and address to:

Magna Print Books
Magna House, Long Preston,
Nr Skipton, North Yorkshire.
England. BD23 4ND.